Heart of Wisdom

G.W. Roberts

DEDICATION

I would like to dedicate this book to my Father who encourages me to find my voice, my Mother who let me focus and helped me along the way, and my Sister who is always here for me no matter what.

I would also like to dedicate this book to the doctors and healthcare providers at BOSTON CHILDREN'S HOSPITAL. I will be donating all the author profits from my book to this hospital.

CONTENTS

"There are stars who's light only reaches the earth long after they have fallen apart. There are people whose remembrance gives light in this world, long after they have passed away. This light shines in our darkest nights on the road we must follow."

Talmud Quote

1 HOME

"Natasha, wake up, its time to get to work, its nearly sunrise actually and mother will yell right now"

"NATASHA! GET DOWN NOW AND FEED THE CHICKENS!"

I run down the creaky gray wooden stairs, while putting my pale yellow shirt on, it's very late and I slept in for an hour!

I am sprinting to get to the barn while my older Brother Alexey giggles, his brownish black hair falling over his eyes. I yell to him that he's not working too.

It's a cold crisp morning. The sun is not up yet, but the sky is starting to lighten. The snows have not come yet, so there is much work to be done.

When I'm at the chicken pen I'm a bit tired and out of breath. I sit down on a stool and the plump reddish orange chickens peck at my worn down leather shoes. They are hungry, so I give them pieces of my bread; another breakfast wasted.

I live in the shtetl village of Nikuda, which is a tiny

village that is full of farmers, bakers, and a few shops here and there. It is full of trees and farms and a lazy river running through the middle of the town. The sunlight always hits the pine needles perfectly so that it leaves a very bright streak of light. Even in the winter, the sun makes the village bright and sparkling. The neighboring town, Mutnyy, is flat and swampy. It has no trees and looks like a barren wasteland. Mutnyy is always muddy and brown, even in winter, when it should be frozen and white. I believe you can always tell when you have met someone from Nikuda rather than Mutny because they are brighter and friendlier.

I look through the barn door and see a figure walking past on the village road in the pre-dawn light. Then I see that it is Vera, the last person in this village I want to talk to. She's a tall girl, thin and pale with curly blonde hair and dark brown eyes. She always seems to be frowning at people and always has something that has annoyed her.

Vera cries out, "Hey Natasha, what are you doing, farm work?! Ewww! I feel bad for you...you know, I can go to school and get a good education!"

I feel like running over and kicking her. " That's great Vera," I call out, "what have you learned lately?"

I'm feeling annoyed as Vera responds, "lots of things, like spelling and grammar, and arithmetic and science. My teacher says I'm an excellent student. For example, let me spell borscht, B-O-R-S-C-H-T, borscht."

I almost barfed, who can't spell a food name?

Vera laughs and calls out, "*zay gesunt* (good-bye) Natasha, gotta go to school!"

When she is out of sight down the road, I yell, "She is such a snob!" and kick the fence post. I ran inside to get a pail to milk the goat, Anna.

While inside the house again, I see David playing with our dog, Yacov. David is two years old and is so lucky that he still gets three more years to play, because you start to work when you are five if you are a boy. I feel sad; he gets to play when I have to work because I am older. Then again, Alexey had to work when I was three.

I am about to leave, but instead I pick David up and into my arms. He starts yawning and soon falls asleep. I almost fall asleep too so I put him in his cradle. He is so cute when he is sleeping; he looks like an angel, the rosy cheeks, the soft brown hair, and the small hands and feet. He is wearing a checkered shirt and little overalls. I notice I have wasted thirty minutes playing with David, so I run outside and into the barn.

Anna the goat is standing there waiting to be milked. As I approach her she bleats loudly. She is waiting and is getting impatient. When I start milking her my head starts filling with questions such as *why does David play? Why am I thinking? Why is Vera so obnoxious? Why don't I get to go to school?* My head is pounding with questions and I am arguing with myself.

"BAAAAAA!" Anna startles me.

I look at the pail and see that it is now full. I pick up the pail and I walk in the house to give it to Mother. It is noon and it is time to make lunch. I already cleaned out the cow manure from the barn, washed the dog, raked the leaves, watered the potatoes, changed David for services, and recited my prayers to read in front of our *shtetl (town)*.

I help mother make some chicken soup as she tells me to peel two potatoes. I gladly oblige and start peeling them. My Mother's chicken soup is famous in the village. David starts crying, saying he's hungry. Some angel. Mother tells me to give David an apple or some fruit. I go to the pantry and pick out a nice red apple. I give him the apple and he clutches it in his tiny hands, looking at it as if it was a tiny world.

The pot is boiling with the delicious smell that only my Mother's soup makes. I close my eyes and breathe in the lovely smells. My Mother is standing over the stove wearing her puffy white and blue shirt with a purple apron tied in the back. Mother is very thin and average height. She likes to hum while she cooks.

My Father walks into the room with a pile of firewood, his breath still fogging from the cold outside. My Father is tall and has jade green eyes and a big full brown beard. He is mostly bald, and has a black yarmulke cap on his head.

I go to the bathroom and I comb my light brown wavy hair and wash my tan face. I also wash the dirt from my hands in the porcelain basin. Father tells me to wear the blue dress our neighbor Svita gave to me. The dress is pretty, but the wool is itchy. Oh well, beggars can't be choosers they say. Does that make us beggars?

When I come down stairs it is time to eat. I see chicken soup, mandelbrot, and cool water set out on our long wooden dinner table. Our house has a low ceiling with thick wooden beams across the top.

I pick David up and put him in his chair. We all say a prayer and start eating. I am hungry because I did not have breakfast and begin slurping some soup. I do not like mandelbrot, so I eat two bowls of chicken soup. I feel very full after that. My Father snaps off a piece of mandelbrot and chews on it appreciatively. Mother is busy cooking the potatoes in the kitchen.

" Father", I say putting down my spoon, "Vera gets to

go to school and I do not, why? You are the rabbi of our village and you could send me to the school, am I wrong?"

"No" he replies cautiously, not sure where I am going with the questions.

"Then why not, I mean she will grow up to be whatever she wants, to study whatever she wants and I will grow to be just a simple farmer."

"Simple farmer" my father says mainly to himself, a smile on his face, "everything is for the best Natasha."

"What?" I say, not understanding.

Alexey glares at me, "he's telling a story, listen!"

"Listen Children, there is a famous Talmud story, you like those Natasha":

There once was a man who needed a place to stay, he had with him a donkey, a chicken, and a dog. He came to a town and asked at the inn if he could stay for a night. The innkeeper shooed him out the door and told him to go away.

"Everything is for the best" he said and went out.

He found a nice field to lay in, but his dog and rooster ran into the forest, he tried finding the dog but had no luck, "everything is for the best" he said and laid on the wet cold forest ground.

The next morning he awoke and he saw the donkey and chicken were gone; wild beasts probably ate them.

"Everything is for the best" he said and started walking away. He soon learned that the town he was planning to stay in was burned and taken for slavery and if he had stayed there he would have probably died, if he still had the rooster, dog and donkey they would have made noise and he would have been captured, if not that, then eaten. "Everything is for the best" he said and headed home.

I think about the story a moment and then hesitantly say, "I still do not understand Father, how does that relate to me?"

"Well Natasha, you say that farm work is worse than school work, and Vera will be more successful, but maybe you will become a rich successful farmer, am I wrong?"

"No, that might be possible", I offer weakly, knowing better than to disagree.

"Exactly, see!" Father says smiling, "Now with that, lets get to the synagogue, I seem to have two little helpers today!"

I smile weakly, it seems we are done discussing the school topic again.

"Hey! wha about ME!!" David screeches

"Oh yes I forgot, three little helpers," David grins and hugs Father.

"Hmmm... But before you get to be a helper you need to wash your mouth." said Mother. I pick David up and carry him into the bathroom.

"NO!! I NO WHA WASH!! NOOO!!!!" David cries out, struggling and almost knocking over the basin of water.

"Quit squirming runt, and let me get potato off your nose!"

Mother walks in and wipes it off. She says she will deal with David and I should help Father.

I run downstairs and help Father put his kippa on straight. He is bald and starts laughing when it slips off his head. Over the kippa he put on a large black hat, like all the men in the village wears. Father's green eyes glitter beneath the brim of the hat. Everyone wears mostly black clothing. I wonder if there is a village where everyone wears green or blue? Maybe out beyond the dark forest there are villages with purple or red colored outfits. I laugh to myself thinking that.

We finally get out of the house and walk over to the synagogue, the place is loud and talkative. It is definitely a full house tonight. Father walks up and onto the beama, his large tallis draping about him like a cape.

"*A gutntog* (Hello) everyone! It seems to me we have lots here today!"

We start the services and sing prayers, and in two hours I go up to lead a prayer with David. I sing loud and clear, but David just mumbles and stares at everyone. He does not know any prayers yet since he is so little, but everyone probably thinks he is cute. Then I see Vera who is laughing at David. The nerve of her!

I look around for an empty seat. Men sit in the main section and women are separated into the small area to the right. Some women don't attend but stay home to do cooking. In some synagogues women have to sit in an upstairs section that is always hot and stuffy, so I figure our setup is better.

The only seat open is next to Vera. Maybe everyone dislikes her, too. I plop down next to her, not saying hello. She is frowning as usual.

"Nice brother you have!" she whispers icily.

"What's your problem?" I hiss at her.

"You at the moment!" she responds.

Wow, that hurts! Why is she always being so mean? She starts to get up to walk away, smiling coldly. I almost punch her but instead I pinch her arm quickly. She winces then pinches me even harder on my upper arm. No one sees that except for Alexey. He glares at Vera and grabs me, taking me outside.

"What is the matter with you? Fooling around in Shul?" he yells, wiping away tears from my face.

I tell him the whole thing. He is seventeen and knows how to deal with these things. He tells me not to lose my temper like that. I nod between sobs. As we walk out of the synagogue, I see Vera look at me as if I was on her death list. I walk away sticking my tongue out at her.

I hold Alexey's hand even more tightly. As we walk into the house, I run up the stairs and into my room. I feel horrible about pinching her in the synagogue, and my arm still stings where she pinched me. I feel angry at Vera and I'm still upset that I don't get to go to school. Life is so unfair!

I wished I could redo that hour of time, redo what just happened in my life. I lie down and try to close my eyes, but I'm too upset to sleep.

There is a tap on my door, "Come in!" I say.

The door opens and Alexey sticks his head in and says, "Hi Natasha, just seeing if you were okay."

" Yes," I sigh, "I'm fine." I'm not sure if I believe what I said myself.

"Well you sound a little sad. Is it because of the synagogue incident with that Vera girl? Put that behind you, it was not that bad!" He says with a wave of his hand as if to dispel the incident.

He leans forward and says conspiratorially, "I had done a lot worse when I was your age. I punched a friend in the face, and knocked two teeth out. Sadly, he's never talked to me since!"

I want to giggle, but I keep a straight face, "all your telling me is that I have a dumbo as my brother."

He laughs, "that wasn't dumb, that was mean, but something dumb? Ha! Let me think…well, one time, when cousin Joshua came over, I let him hold you, then, when he gave you back to me, I totally let you slip and fall to the ground. That was scary, but luckily we were over the table and you landed in the big bowl of mashed potatoes. Then you started laughing and the whole room laughed."

I sigh, "I thought this story was supposed to be dumb."

" It was, kind of?" he smiles.

"No, it wasn't" I say crossly.

"Get some sleep, everything will seem less dramatic in the morning!" he says smiling.

He leaves my room quietly. As I lie down I think, maybe, just maybe I am going to become a successful farmer, and I fall asleep after tossing and turning.

.

2 THE CZAR

The Czar's men are coming to our town today to collect taxes. No one wants them to come, but wishing they would leave us alone is like wishing it would never snow.

The Czar is the ruler of Russia. I would say he is an unfair man because he should not tax us so much. There is a painting of him Vera showed us all. He looked very ugly. He had greasy pulled back hair and thick eyebrows. His face was very thin and he had a thick, stiff collar around his neck. Each one of his shoulders looked like it had a giant golden mop on it, as if they were being cleaned. His jacket was covered in buttons and sashes with many ribbons strung from one place to another and medals hung everywhere on his chest. There were enough medals for every war we had fought, and we seemed to always be in a lot of wars.

I always wonder why he is our leader. He really doesn't do much for Nikuda except take our money. If I could choose our leader he would have to be wise like my father, kind like my brothers, and caring like my mother.

My father was almost drafted into the army but luckily he fell and broke his knee. I wonder if Alexey will go into a pointless war. The soldiers say the wars are for the glory of Russia. I don't like the thought of Alexey risking his life for Russia. It seems to me that they forget about the smaller towns until they need more money or soldiers for war. I hardly even know why we are fighting these wars. Maybe the Czar has an empty patch on his chest and needs to cover it with a medal.

I get out of bed and start to change. I dump my face into the washbasin. Splash! The water is cold against my face.

I think about the year before when I accidentally bumped into a solider, Captain Vladislav. He was tall and muscular, and had short blond hair. His jawline was angular and he had nicely contoured cheeks. The most striking part of him, however, was his brilliant, blue eyes. The issue was that these beautiful eyes were also somehow cold and had an eerie darkness to them. He once gave me a cruel look and twisted my wrist. But it could have been worse. He could have killed me. That memory gives me the shivers. I always try not to think of that day. I am afraid of the Czar's men, as father has talked about how horrible they are. It was said that if you have a ruble less of taxes than you should, they would kill you. At least ten people went to jail because they couldn't pay their taxes.

"Children hide under your bed, they are here, the soldiers are here!" father yells, snapping me out of my trance.

Father runs to the door, looking nervous, while mother tells me to go into David's room to hide. I see that Alexey is already in David's room, sitting on the floor cross-legged. He also looks nervous, but I can see he is trying to hide that. Mother hugs us all, telling us that everything will be okay and not to worry.

I hear heavy boots tromp in and a few demanding voices. I hear shouting downstairs, something about too little money. The more the shouting, the more I feel scared. I feel like I want to cry, but I know that would not solve anything. I hug mother tighter and she whispers, "it's okay, Father's almost done."

I can tell she feels reluctant saying that. It is an odd sensation in that her hugs make me feel warm and safe, but I am old enough to know how much danger we are in.

Finally, there is a slam at the door, a long silent pause, and a long sigh of relief from Father.

I run downstairs, overjoyed, and hug Father. He practically collapses into his easy chair. He says, "everything is okay", then he says something about how kind that man was. "Corporal Checkov was tired and he let us have five rubles less, and he didn't kill me!"

I giggle, but it was a giggle of relief not mirth. I gave my Father a big hug.

"Why Papa?" I whisper, "Why did he give us a break on our taxes?"

"Because perhaps he's a friend."

Does a Cossack know what that word means I wonder?

"Okay Papa!" David says. I hug David, he seems kind of shaken up. He runs upstairs with our small dog Yacov because the dog makes him happy.

The rest of us all sat there for a while, until Alexey stands up,

"I believe they are gone, I mean the Czars men, and I have got to go sweep Mrs. Flitz's chimney, so... zay gesunt! (Good bye)."

He runs out the door throwing his arms in his coat. He heads towards the barn where he keeps his chimney sweep tools.

I go into my room and I pull a book off of my overflowing bookshelf. I pick out one of my favorite books, one that my Father gave me about mythological stories and creatures. It tells tales of creatures like Baba Yaga, the witch who has a house with chicken legs at the bottom, or the Slavic Dragon, who had three heads instead of one, and Buyan, the island which appears and disappears mysteriously. When there are stressful times, which seem to happen a lot in my little village, I like to escape into a little world of my books. I finish one of the stories and close the book, setting it down on my nightstand, and then I run to the window to look outside. A few snowflakes fall on my quiet town. I hear Mother humming in the kitchen as she cooks. The house is warm and I am glad we are safe and sound for now.

.

3 KATYA ZUKOV

The next morning I get up early. I walk into the bathroom, look in the mirror and see I still have a small bruise on my upper arm where Vera had pinched me. I walk into Alexey's room and see him sitting at the windowsill.

"Hey Alexey!" I whisper.

"What! Oh, it's you Natasha; did you see the bruise on your arm? It looks like a big bee sting."

"Yes," I grumble, " Alexey, is it very noticeable?"

"A little, but most people will just think you forgot to wash like usual, or you can wear long sleeves. Don't worry about it. Lets go make breakfast."

We walk downstairs and get a couple eggs from the chicken pen. He puts them in the boiling water.

"Natasha, its a cold November, right?"

"Yes, I believe so." I respond.

" Today I have to clean more chimneys, and fireplaces." Alexey is the town chimneysweeper. This is a good profession, but I know my Father had hoped he would also want to be a Rabbi like him. Maybe this is why I always want to go to school. Father always said women could not be rabbis. A woman being a rabbi is like an orange on the Passover Seder plate he always said.

The fire crackles and burns the log. We say nothing for a few minutes.

"BOOOO!" shouts David waddling into the room and laughing, Alexey and me jump.

" David, don't do that!" I scold.

"Lets PLAY!!" he screams, jumping in circles and rolling on the floor.

"Do you only know how to scream?" I ask.

"NOOO!" he shouts.

Seems like it I say in my head.

Alexey takes the pot out of the fireplace and takes the eggs out. He gives two to me and one on David's plate, and takes four for himself. I take another one out and eat it.

Mother and Father come downstairs and take some boiled eggs too. "Good morning kids, beautiful day out isn't it?" father says happily. "You beat your parents downstairs!" he says, taking another boiled egg.

"Well, guess what? Tonight someone special is coming for services!" Mother says joyfully.

"Who?" Alexey and I say.

"Katya's family!"

"Yay!" I shout, jumping out of my chair.

Katya was this girl who came every year to visit with her family. Her Father is my Father's oldest friend, so every year they travel from their village to stay at our house.

Alexey groans and says, "No! We cannot let that family visit again! Natasha and Katya talk and whisper and sing loudly all night! I never get a wink of sleep."

15

I giggle and tell him that's his problem, he sighs and looks out the windowsill again.

I head downstairs and start my chores. While I am doing my chores I wonder what Katya looks like now, is her red hair browner now? Does she still only wear dresses? Growing up with two brothers makes a person wish for at least one sister.

KNOCK-KNOCK! My parents rush to the door. I swoop David up and into my room. He squirms a little and fidgets while I put him into a dressy outfit, a white shirt with a tie and black pants, he looks so cute in it. I put a light pink dress on with a matching bow. I like it, father thinks it is beautiful and mother does too. This is also a gift from our neighbor Svita. Alexey comes out wearing a very white shirt with a vest and black pants; he is also wearing black leather boots.

My father opens the door and we see our old family friends the Zukov family. They are all dressed fancy for the occasion. I run over to hug Katya.

"A gutntog Natasha (hello), shoyn langnit gezen! (long time no see!)"

Her hair is still a pretty red, but it is much longer and she had it in a beautiful braided bun. My hair can have braids, but it is too short to make nice braids.

Mother had ready her usual amazing dinner, knishes, chicken soup, babka, challah, and blintz. She gives the kids water and the parent's wine, there are also crackers, cheeses, and fig spread.

Mother and father are talking to Katya's parents; Katya and I pay close attention when her mother was speaking.

"It took us a little longer than expected, the snow was blocking our way and our horse Tulip is sick. I noticed that when we got off the wagon, she was shaking and sneezing, so this might be a little dilemma for our plan on staying.

We may have to stay until our horse recovers."

" That's fine, we always need a little company, right kids?" Mother says.

I nod; it would be fun to have Katya stay. Katya's Father looks worried, "But Katya's school starts the day after we usually leave, then our kid can't go to school!"

Father looks a little disturbed, after the talk we had about going to school. "I am afraid Natasha does not go to school, but I do teach her. That is why you may think she goes to school".

Katya looks at me surprised. She assumed I attended school.

" Oh, that would work, you seem to be quite a teacher Mr. Weinroeber, I thought your kids did go to school, ah, you are a good friend, and a smart man, I am impressed!" says Katya's Father.

Father beams at this compliment and shakes Mr. Zukov's hand. " Thank you, Thank you, may love and happiness always be in your heart" father exclaims. After dinner we say prayers and then dancing, singing and talking. Father even gets out his violin and plays a happy dancing klezmer song. Soon enough, it is time to go to bed.

Alexey went into his room and I lead Katya into mine. She lets down her long hair and then combs it out. Her red hair is so long, it touches midway down her back! She puts a robe on that I lent to her and sits on the blankets and pillow that we made into a makeshift bed. We start talking about home and animals and catch up.

As Katya is petting Yacov, our dog, she asks thoughtfully, " What really annoys you in your village?"

" Vera."

"What's a Vera?"

" A girl named Vera, she comes by our house to get to school, which she brags about. And she pinched my arm hard! Can you believe that?" I say in a flat voice.

Katya looks bewildered, "she pinched you? How come? That was really mean, why would she be so mean?"

" I don't know." I say quietly.

" Yes, perhaps, but pinching you hard! By the way, is that how you got the bruise on your arm?"

"Yes" I grumble, noting that it is the second time someone asked me.

"Why does Vera hate you so much?" Katya asks.

"Well," I begin, "it started seven years ago when we were all playing games in the street, and Alexey was watching us. He was about ten, maybe eleven. Anyway, we were playing out side near the synagogue. It was after the morning service. We were all playing tag. I was "it" and I started chasing Pytor, but he was too fast. Instead, I started to chase Vera and, when I tagged her, I accidently pushed her and she fell into the gravel, staining her new fancy white dress. She got so mad and yelled at me. I told her that it was an accident. Daniel and Denis, the twins, started laughing at her. She walked over, screamed in their face and stomped on each of their feet. Vera always had a bad temper, like her Father the village Mayor."

Katya shakes her head, "No, I don't think anyone would hate someone for doing that, what else could it be?"

I hesitate, "Well, I guess that's not the only reason she is not my friend. Something happened when I was maybe eight. This is when she really started hating me. We were walking together and I asked if she liked my new skirt. Vira said it made me look fat, so I called her an idiot."

"That's silly to be mad about, is there more? There must be something you don't want to remember or don't want to talk about!" Katya says probing me.

I sigh, Katya knows me pretty well.

"Okay, fine. I guess she hates me because about a year

ago I was taking a little walk around the field near the edge of town. That field borders on the dark forest. I thought I heard something rustle in the nearby forest edge, so I thought maybe it was a small animal. I grabbed a stick and tossed it into the woods. When I threw that stick, wouldn't you know it, but Vera has to walk over with her dog Sali. The stupid dog had to run after the stick right into the dark forest. I saw Vera run after the dog, yelling for Sali to stop. About ten meters away from the edge of the dark forest Vera was too afraid to proceed. All our parents had told us bad things about being in the dark forest."

"Oy!" Katya says sympathetically.

I continue, "Vera whipped around and started to march over with steam coming out of her ears. She said, 'you filthy good for nothing dirt bag! Go and retrieve my dog!'"

I pause remembering that day clearly now.

"I replied to her with a flat tone that I was flattered she would leave that responsibility to me, but that there was no way I was running into the dark forest at dusk."

I sigh at the memory. I suppose I have made myself forget that day, which I still felt guilty about.

I continue, "Vera had screamed and pleaded with me to get her dog for her. She was crying like her dog died, which actually it probably did. Then I left her crying alone at the forest edge and ran home and told my dad what had happened. He was a bit proud that I did not go in the dark woods, but a bit mad that I made Vera cry. He told me to apologize to her, so of course I did. Vera would not accept my apology. That's pretty much the summary of my Vera hating business."

"Well, why didn't you just go into the dark woods? So many people in all the surrounding villages are so afraid, but how many have actually gone in and seen scary stuff? If this was my dog, or little Yacov here", Katya says petting my dog lovingly, "I would have gone in to save him. I mean really, the woods near my home have great berries, mushrooms, and wild flowers! I bet you guys are missing out because of superstition and fear!"

I shrug, "Hey, its not the woods I'm afraid of, it's the things in the woods, the things that go bump in the night that I'm afraid of."

Katya smirks, "What are you saying? Were Russian girls! When things go bump in the night," she bangs her fist on the floor, "we bump back."

I smile, "ooh, your so brave! Weren't you the one who was afraid of the spider in the bathroom? As I recall, I was the one who had to 'bump' that spider for you!"

Katya frowns, "Hey! It was big, furry and I was pretty sure it had poison fangs! I'm sure that spider is the scariest thing I will ever experience for the rest of my life!"

"So you could admit that I saved your life, but who will save you from… the pillow monster!"

I throw my pillow at her and it hits her in the face. Katya then hits me hard in the stomach with her pillow. We parry blows from the pillows for a while until we are both reeling.

I shout, "Do you surrender?"

"Not on your life!" Katya laughs.

I yell, "Then prepare… for pillow destruction!"

"Kids, get to sleep! Its already late!" Mother enters the room and blows out my candle on the nightstand. Katya and I pull on our covers. It's like having a sister. I fall quickly into a dreamy sleep, my stomach full and feeling content.

4 PLAY TIME

For breakfast we have thick slices of black bread with honey and some strawberries. Katya is wearing a light green shirt with overalls. Her hair is in a regular ponytail. I have my hair in braids, my golden highlights shining above my light brown hair. I am wearing a white top with regular grey pants. Mother gives each of us coats and tells us to go outside and play. We run outside and start chasing each other down the streets.

It is cold outside, I feel that sense that winter is approaching. The sky is a mix of clouds, with some darker clouds to the west. My father said growing a lot of your own food is a recipe for happiness; you can smile when the sun shines and smile when the rain is watering your plants. That makes me think about some of the chores around the house I have to do later. My parents are giving me more time to play though because of our guests.

Midway through a game of 'Cossack in the middle', Vera

wanders by. As usual, she wears a fine embroidered floral dress, her curly blond hair pulled back with a fancy hairpin.

"Hey Natasha! Oh, so you got a friend," she says motioning to Katya, "her name is...?"

" Kovitiva. She is royalty from Moscow." I say sternly.

"I..um..what?" Katya stammers.

"Play along with me here", I whisper to her.

She nods, catching on.

Vera looks disapprovingly, "Kovitiva, man, you have long red hair, were you from, hair town?"

Katya smirks, "No, and for your reference, I am the cousin of the Czar, and I was sent to this town to see if reports were true, that mean people in this town were picking on others. Now, if you excuse me for a moment, let me inform my messenger about you." says Katya.

Vera runs away, but before she does that she pushes me over. I fall over and land with a thud. Katya helps me up and asks, "What is her problem?"

" That's Vera for you", I say and peer in her direction, and "I don't think she has many friends, unless you count her snobby brother Elliot."

She helps me stand up and we keep walking.

Katya says, "your so soft to people, you should really stand up for yourself more! But I'm one to talk, I don't know if I would be brave enough in a scary situation."

"I hope nether of us have to test that " I say. "Besides, according to Father, all I will be is a simple farmer."

Katya reacts," maybe you shouldn't let other people define you, like Vera does. How can you ignore her, she just pushed you over! How do you do this?"

I look at her silently, letting her words sink in.

She sighs, "I'm sorry. It's just that your such a strong person, you should be more confident."

"Thanks"

We keep walking and then I turn around and show her our barn. Our barn is small compared to the others in the village. It is reddish in color and needs a new coat of paint. The upper part of the barn is storage for hay and seeds. The lower part has two cows and a few goats in pens. I bring Katya over to one of the goats to milk.

" This is Anna, she is very nice and her milk is delicious", I say as I drag over a pail. I squeeze some milk out and let Katya try. She gets the milk all over her. I laugh and she starts protesting that I have done this for years and she only just tried it today. Her protests made me laugh more.

Alexey walks over. When he sees Katya, her hair wet with the milk, he laughs too.

She starts yelling at him, angrily. I feel bad and should put a stop to this.

" STOP THIS YELLING!!" I snap at both of them. They stop.

Katya walks next to me, "now, Alexey, say sorry" I begin

"Sorry" Alexey whispers,

"Katya?"

"Sorry Alexey for yelling at you"

Alexey walks away, chuckling, "and to think Babushka always tries to scare us with folk stories about winter wolves, you two are like your own wolf pack!"

"It's getting cold Natasha, lets go inside", says Katya.

We gather the pail of milk and collect more eggs from the chickens. We then head inside to the house.

This is the last day that Katya will stay. Their horse, Tulip, is now better and they are leaving. I am sad that my friend will be leaving.

We ate a light lunch of dark rye bread with blackberry jam and dried apricots. We sang more songs, and hugged each other.

They plan to leave an hour before dinner to get some travel under way before the sun sets, so we pack them a dinner and some fruit and snacks. I wave good-bye as their horse and wagon trot down the road. I watch as it recedes down the road. Katya has to get back to go to school, which reminds me again that I won't be going to school. I would have to keep teaching myself from Alexey's text books and books from my father's library.

I am sad my friend left. Even little David seems sad. I suppose he loved all the attention. Oh well, too bad for him. When I return to my room I see that Katya forgot her gold earrings! They were left over by the washbasin on my dresser. Oh well, I thought, she will come back next year.

5 BABUSHKA'S STORY

At last it is winter, the time when my Babushka (Grandma) comes to visit. Since Katya and her family went back to their village several boring months have passed, filled with nothing but chores on the farm and reading book after book at night. I have read most of Alexey's books twice and even 'borrowed' some texts from Papa's study. I am bored and cannot wait for Babushka to visit. I wait at the window and shift around anxiously.

"Papa, when will she be here, you said at ten but its already ten minutes after ten!"

Papa smiles, and says, "its okay, I am sure she is fine, but with this time we can clean the house."

Papa nudges me out of my chair and tells me to get moving. Reluctantly I walk up the stairs and into my room.

When I reach my room I start to survey it. My Bookshelf is cluttered with books and Talmud stories and my desk has many papers scattered. My mirror has a few clothes next to it and a sock hanging from the top of the mirror. I sit down and sigh, well, it's been messier.

David waddles in, "hello! I am a goosie! Quack-quack!" He waddles out. I laugh. His room is way cleaner, but that's only because my mother cleans it. He just plays, and honestly, at the age of two, what do you really own? All you need is your diaper and a blanket and your good to go!   I bend over putting items on the shelf.

My room may not be as clean as Alexey's room, but Alexey's job is cleaning. Yes, cleaning chimneys, but who would hire a messy chimneysweeper? Alexey's room used to be a clutter of books when he was in school, but I slowly borrowed them, and he never asked for them back. He helped me through the tough parts in the readings. He's such a great brother. Even though Alexey and I are very close, I have never understood why he chose to become a chimneysweeper instead of a rabbi. That decision sure didn't make my father happy.

I creep out of my room and near the stairs. I can hear murmuring about Babushka but I really cannot hear what they were saying. All I can hear is "oh, this is so annoying, my mother is going to tell the children durachok stories and mess up their minds!"

I think about what will happen when she sees David. Maybe she will forget about me and just care about David. I shake my head- that will never happen.

"Natasha, come down, I need your help!" I run down the stairs, which makes a creak every time I step, and join my mother.

"I need you to make some mashed potatoes. Now! Lets get moving, your Babushka could be here any minute now!"

I murmur, "That's what you said forty minutes ago"

I grab the potatoes and get down to business. For an

hour, I am mashing, mixing and adding spices to the mashed potatoes. I plop down on the sofa to rest, just when the door opens with an arctic blast and Alexey comes in from the cold. He visibly shivers.

I ask, "what were you doing outside in the cold, it's colder than the Czar's heart! More importantly, why do you have no coat?"

He shivers and sneezes loudly, "A boy, about nine years old, was outside with only a few shmatas (rags) to wear. He was alone and looked to be homeless. The least I could do was give him my coat."

He ran upstairs and I can hear him cough and sneeze. I sigh and sit down in a comfy chair next to the fireplace. Before I know it I doze off.

Later, I wake up quickly and stare at the top of the window and into the sky. The sun was past mid-day. I stand up and run to the window, I can see a figure approaching near the house. I can see an old woman on a horse drawn wagon that stops next to our house. I can tell it is Babushka!

I run to the door and open it, and there she is! On her is a royal blue scarf with a pretty yellow pattern on it. She is wearing a faded green coat and a teal dress with a sunflower design. She hugs everyone. She walks inside, dusts the snow off and sits down next to me.

"Hello Natasha! How are you this year my sweet potato?" she says with a crinkly but sweet voice.

"I am good, you must be wondering where my brother is, well brothers, I have another brother now!"

Babushka looks at me delighted, "so I heard in the letters! Might I see him?"

I nod, "Yeah, I guess, but he's napping, so you have to be quiet, okay?"

We walk upstairs and see David sleeping, Mother is in

Alexey's room cleaning.

I ask Babushka to wait with David well I checked with Alexey.

I hear loud coughing from Alexey. It is sort of a harsh, hacking cough, like a dog's bark. I am a little scared; maybe he has caught Dragon Cough, which several unfortunate people in the village have been suffering from. It is a terrible thought that I push out of my mind.

I walk into his room cautiously. Mother is giving him some herbal medicine. He is a bit red in the face as he keeps coughing.

"Hey Alexey, are you ok? I just came in because Babushka is here..."

"Leave, tell her I'm sick!" he says in a raspy voice.

I retreat out of the door, walking back into David's room, where Babushka is holding David, rocking him, and slowly singing to him.

"Oh, Babushka, I don't want to be rude, but, maybe you can tell me a folk story, you don't have to but, please?"

"Ah my sweet Natasha, firm and gentle, just like me when I was your age. I was hoping you would ask, my sweet potato."

We go downstairs and sit down at the dinner table. David wakes up just in time, his eyes wide and eager. I plop into one of the comfy chairs to listen. The sun is setting giving the room a warm glow and the snow is softly patting the window.

"Now, I will tell a story! Gather around kids! Once in the town of Mutnyy, I was getting a pitcher of water from the shtetl's well. I felt like someone was watching me. You know that feeling?"

I nod my head, caught up in the story.

"I heard whispers all around, like children telling a secret to each other. It was frightening but I kept telling myself, relax there is nothing there but the wind in the trees."

David snuggles up tighter against Babushka, his eyes wide.

Babushka continues, "I dragged the bucket up from the deep dark well. I felt the sense of a presence and a rustling sound like old dried leaves crinkling under a boot, so I suddenly looked up. In front of me had suddenly appeared a strange woman. She was very pale and beautiful, but there was something about her that scared me. In a whisper she said, 'Young child, you look tired, let me help you.' I wanted to say no and run away, but her diamond eyes made me nod and give her the bucket. Then when she looked inside of it and she gave the pail back to me cautiously, as if the water would kill her or something. I looked at her intensely, waiting for her reaction."

"Ok, I think you can do this alone. This world is not for the weak." she said with an uneasy grin. Just as I began to walk away I heard her talking again, but to someone else. I turned around and saw she was with another young girl from the village. She leaned down to give the child a hug, but then I saw she bared shiny white fangs and was biting the child! I saw the child turn from peach to white, it was the most frightening thing I ever saw!"

" That's enough!" My father cuts her off, angrily. "Stop telling the children your Babushka stories! It will give them nightmares!"

I walked away, as I did not want to argue with father. I heard Babushka reply angrily, "But it is all true! It actually happened to me!"

My father snapped back at her, "If it really happened, why did you not tell me this story when I was a child!"

She stays quiet, but I could hear her whisper to herself, "because in uneasy dreams I sense that things that sleep must some day awaken."

I go up to my room and get into bed. It is a long time until I fall into an uneasy sleep thinking on what those words might mean

6 THANKING SVITA

I slowly walk up to the big house in the middle of the street. I know it is strange to walk up to my frienemy's house, but I also know that the mother of this rotten apple is surprisingly a kind gentle soul. Usually my mother would go instead of me, but I insisted this time on thanking Svita for the clothing she gave to me.

The Hingleffer live on the other side of town from our home, down a tree lined road past the town square. Mr. Hingleffer was the town mayor, so his house is a short walk to the small town hall where he seems to be always at work. I slowly walk up the steps to the big house. The exterior coat of the wooden house was a beige-yellow color, and the pathway is brick with an ornate pattern. The entrance has two flowerpots, and the door is white with a golden brass doorknocker. The family name Hingleffer is displayed in bronze letters. I hesitantly knock on the door, while jumping up and down in the cold. Slowly, the door opens and out steps a man dressed in fine clothes. He has a crinkled face and a few white hairs on the top of his head. He stands up straight like an army man.

"Who are you?" he asks in a very formal and deep voice. I don't remember the man's name, but I remember that he is always doing errands for the Hingleffer family in town.

I answer, "I am Natasha, I am here to see Svita Hingleffer, to thank her for the clothes she gave me. Who are you?"

"I am Victor, the house keeper."

"Pleased to meet you Mister Victor! This sure looks like a big house to take care of. It looks lovely on the outside."

"Why, thank you, that is so kind of you. Please come in and judge the inside, if you would be so kind." He gestures for me to come in.

When I step inside, I almost slip. I look at the floor and see that it is shiny smooth polished wood, not pine brown weathered wood like we have in our house.

"I will get Mrs. Hingleffer right away" he says.

I look around at the inside of the room. The wall is sweet red mahogany with many paintings of the Hingleffer family. I see several paintings of Vera and a few of her older brother Elliot, both looking serious. Are you not allowed to smile in a portrait? There is a formal picture of Mayor Hingleffer with the Czar, they both look cold and serious.

The chair I am sitting in is cushiony; it was softer than my bed! The ceiling is painted white with a small chandelier hanging above. The house is way nicer than I even thought it would be, Mayor Hingleffer must be doing well with his job.

Suddenly, Victor is tapping my shoulder, "ahem, Miss Natasha, please follow me to the dining room."

I slowly get up from the chair and walk carefully to the dining room. As I am walking I notice the smell of pine turning into the smell of lavender. I walk into the room with Victor following me and he leads me to sit into yet another even more comfortable chair.

Svita is sitting straight up in her chair across from me at a rosewood dining table with deep inlaid carvings around the edge. I was a bit perplexed on why we had to have a conference of just saying thank you. I quickly scoot up and cross my legs lady-like as mother had shown me. I make a slight cough to get her attention.

Svita opens her mouth and says, "Are you sick also?"

I answer back "What? Oh no, are you?"

She gives a slight nod and says, "I do believe I have a small cold, so I am sitting across from you. If I was well, I would sit next to you."

I nod in understanding. There was an uncomfortable silence as the small clock in the dining room ticks. Then I realize she is wondering why I am here so I announce, "thank you so much for the clothes you gave to me, they fit very well!"

"Ah yes, you see Vera is tall for her age and could not fit in the clothes anymore, so I suspected you would."

I look at the floor. She continues. "You always seem to be full of light and energy, but some of your clothing, how should I put it, they are so out of style?"

I blush scarlet red, "I suppose you are right, fashion is not a top priority on a small family farm."

"I understand perfectly. When I was a farm girl, I would wear my 'yesterday clothes' if that were the first thing I saw in the morning to wear. When I was a teenager, oh so many years ago, I once woke to the sound of songbirds. I stretched, and walked to my wardrobe. I looked outside and saw that it was just so beautiful; I just had to wear my only nice dress. I went to the market to get my mother some eggs and butter. After I got there I bumped into a tall

33

blond man. He had a very mean look on his face."

She blew her nose in the middle of the story, and then continued, " but when he saw me he smiled. I looked up to see the former mayor's son Pytor Hingleffer. As I looked into his lovely steel grey eyes, and he looked into mine, I knew it was true love at first sight. He looked at me and smiled, "You have a lovely dress young lady, and it is like spring itself." I blushed, and said, "Thank you, my name is Svita"

He winked, "I am going to have to remember that name."

She began to have a large coughing fit, which abruptly ended her reminiscing. "Are you alright?" I said concerned. "Maybe I should get going, you seem tired."

I got up and start to head for the door when Svita stops me, "wait, you forgot something"

She goes back in the dining room and picks up a box, "you may need this"

I take the box and open it, inside is a box of beautiful blue and red sweaters, two lovely beige coats, two pairs of corduroy pants, a beautiful azure blue dress and a striped woven hat.

"I knit the sweaters myself, but Vera didn't care for them. She prefers the fancy ones Pytor brings back from visits to St.Petersburg." she mentions.

My eyes start to water, it is not even my birthday yet and I am getting a pretty new wardrobe! I say thank you twice and go out the door carrying the clothes.

I walk through the town carrying my clothes with a big smile on my face. When I go up to my front door carrying this bundle, Mother opens it. When she sees the box of clothes in my hands she looks stunned.

"Did you thank her or beg for more clothes?" she asks

skeptically.

I laugh, "she just gave them to me. I guess a very early birthday present?"

She looks a little suspicious, then softens and says, "Okay, but then go do your chores."

I know Mother is not happy about me bringing back more gifted clothing, but they are so pretty. I smile and put the clothes in my room, happy and satisfied.

.

7 KATYA IS MISSING

I wake up to the voice of my father and mother talking to each other downstairs, but something about their tone makes me have an uneasy sense. I slowly walk down the stairs and peek into the kitchen. Mom has on her usual apron and is by the corner of the counter top, and Papa is near the stove gripping a letter in his hand against his chest. They have worried faces. Mother's eyes are tearing up. I feel suddenly uneasy, was I in trouble?

Part of my brain wants me to run away, and part is searching for what I could have done wrong, and the other part isn't even waiting for the others, it is inventing excuses and apologies for whatever was wrong.

I walk into the room and they stop talking. "Mother? What's going on?"

My parents look at each other in worry, and Mother starts to speak. " Natasha there's no easy way of saying this but Katya's parents sent us a letter and-"

I snatch the letter from the table and read it quickly, it

reads:

Dear Mr. and Mrs. Wienrober,
I have devastating news. Katya is missing, she went to the edge of
the forest to pick berries, but after four hours she did not come back.
It has been a week now, and by the time this letter reaches you it will
already be at least three weeks. We searched all over town but we
could not find her. We miss her so much.
Sincerely,
The Zukov Family

I am devastated, my best friend, Katya, is missing! My lip
starts to quiver but I can't hold myself in. I start sobbing. I
slide down onto the ground and cry like a little baby. My
mother puts her arm around me to comfort me but I still
keep crying. I grab onto mother, clutching her white dress
in my hand.

She smooths her hand across my back and says, "Shhh,
its okay, its okay!"

I am still crying. I run to my room and slam the door, sit
on my bed and continue to cry. My brain is spinning and I
have no train of thought. I am so upset. I stuff my face in
my pillow and my shoulders heave with crying.

There is a knock on the door, so I groan, "Come in"

The door creaks open and little David walks in quietly,
"are you okay?"

I nod, "I am just a little upset, Katya went missing, you
know the girl with the pretty long red hair that came by
recently."

He sat down on my lap and says, "Oh, I liked that girl."

I sniff, "I liked her too David, I liked her too."

David hugs me, "will you tell me a story?"

I smile "maybe later."

David snuggles into my arms; I rock him until he falls asleep. I walk into his room and put him in his tiny bed. He rolls over and starts to breathe a steady pace. I place his baby blue blanket on him and smile. He is so soft and full of hope. I would bet that when he grows up, he will be a smart, well-educated young man-maybe living in America. I tiptoe near Alexey's room and hear him wheeze as he sleeps. I turn around and behind me was my mother looking angry, "And what do you think your doing?"

I swallow hard, "I just wanted to check on Alexey, I'm worried"

She frowns, "and this brother of yours is sick, I told you twice not to go near his room, but no matter how many times I tell you to stop, you still don't listen, he might have a dangerous sickness and get you ill, do you really want that to happen?"

I shake my head no, my eyes wide. She seems to be pretty upset over a little cold. Was it a worse cold than it seemed?

She sighs, "then go to your room immediately! Read a book or something."

I walk back to my room and lay down, still devastated about Katya. The sun is setting over Nikuda. The village looks so peaceful yet it stirs with sadness. It is a lovely village and I make a silent prayer that I will never have to leave. Father always said that sleep is a good cure for sadness, and that sometimes you awake to find problems have resolved by themselves. Perhaps tomorrow things will improve. It is a comforting thought to think that things can't get worse off from here. I cling to that thought tightly and fall to sleep eventually.

8 DRAGON COUGH

My mother scheduled an appointment with the local doctor, Alstirch Misher. He is two hours late and all I can do is sit there and listen to Alexey cough his lungs out. It started from an occasional cough but has turned into a full bark. After about an hour I get very frustrated but I know the doctor will come some time soon. I can hear Alexey throwing up into a bucket. I feel helpless.

My mom is the only one who is allowed in his room, and even then she wears a thick scarf tightly wrapped around her mouth and nose. She also wears her planting gloves and gardening apron. She told Father to take care of David, so he put him in his overalls facing forward as if he was attached to him. David screeches in delight at the sight of this new perspective and claps his hands. I smirk; good luck getting him back to the ground.

A tapping at the door announces that the doctor has arrived. Father opens the door and shakes the old man's hand.

"Doctor Misher, thank you so much for coming"

He nods gravely, "I am so sorry about my delay, many people in the town are sick, Henry, Jacob, Rosetta, Svita…"

I gasp, not Svita also! What was causing this tragedy?

My father breaks my train of thought, "Yes, my son is right up here, usually he is a hearty boy, but a few hours after stupidly being out in the cold without a jacket, he grew ill."

Doctor Misher strokes his chin, "most unfortunate, shall we take a look?" My father nods.

We walk upstairs into Alexey's room and the doctor puts on a pair of long gloves and takes a good look at him and scratches his chin. Then he inspects Alexey's ears, eyes, and throat.

The doctor sighs, "I am afraid that Alexey has been one of many to fall under the horrid Dragon Cough, and I have no medicine to cure this. The only slim chance he has is if he has the strength and luck to pull through. But I have to warn you that I have buried ten people just this week. Actually, only a very few people have survived this sickness so far, so keep the healthy children away from him."

Mother starts to cry, "don't you have anything to cure my child?"

He shakes his head, "although our medical knowledge is very advanced, we have no idea of what causes these illnesses or how to stop them. We probably will never know. It is a deep mystery that only God knows. I have heard from one of the rabbis, in the village on the other side of the dark forest, that there may be some magic potion cure for dragon cough, but to be honest that sounds ridiculous"

My father sniffs, he seems about to tear up, so the doctor speaks again, "if it makes you feel any better, some matters of life and death are God's territory where we dare not tread."

I stand at the edge of the door trying not to cry. I feel a stone in the back of my throat and a pain goes down my chest. Why is everything so horrible? First, Katya missing, then Alexey gets sick.

What did I do wrong God? What did I do wrong?

Was it because I fought with Vera during services? Was it because I keep bugging father to go to school? Am I the reason why two people dear to me have their lives in jeopardy, or in Katya's case, already likely gone?

I push the thought to the back of my mind, but at the same time realize this must be true, that it is my fault and I have to fix this in any way I can.

The next morning I wake to the sound of my brother's sneezing, coughing and hacking. I feel like I just have to get out of the house! I throw my weathered blue shirt on and a pair of wrinkled pants. I look at the nice outfits Svita gave me but decide not to wear them because I am worried I would ruin them. I though to myself, I might as well never wear them ever because I am not even wearing them when I have no chores to do! I step out of the house door and breath in the smell of pine and fresh snow, oh do I love that smell. I head down the village road towards the center of our small village.

As I walk down the village road, I glance at all the houses that have wooden signs reading 'DRAGON COUGH, ENTER AT OWN RISK'. I remember that Svita had Dragon Cough, poor her, her kids probably are whining constantly giving her even more stress. Then it occurs to me that she is the mayor's wife and the wife of the mayor probably can afford an expert doctor in Dragon Cough. Maybe, the Hingleffer family could let us use one of their fancy doctor experts or at least let me know if they have found some rare cure!

I run to their house like a rabbit with the scent of fresh

carrot in front of its nose. I have many distractions along the way. I see Harry, the pushcart vendor yelling, "hot steamed babka for sale! Warm sticky buns! Half off!" Maybe he knows that babka is my favorite food so he is trying to tempt me into buying some. I have my heart set on going to Vera's house and I'm not going to let half off babka pull me away from my goal.

Tatiana, the seamstress, is in her shop setting up a dress on a mannequin. As I near the shop I see just how lovely the dress is. It is a pale apricot colored dress with lace around the shoulders. The sleeves are translucent with a beautiful pattern that is hardly visible. The waist has a golden silk belt with a bow that shimmers every time she moves it. The bottom of the dress is crenelated and has a delicate lace hem. I walk up to the window to get a closer look. But whom am I kidding? I can never afford a dress like that…only the people in Vera's neighborhood wear those dresses. Oh wait, I realize I got distracted a bit and keep on walking at a steady pace to Vera's house. I walk further until I am at Vera's fancy house.

When I get there, I knock on the door and wait. Victor opens the door, and I see he is holding a cup of steaming water. He looks like he has not had much sleep lately.

"Miss Natasha, a pleasure seeing you again, but, I must warn you, Mrs. Hingleffer is sick and is so very contagious. So please let me know why must your presence come to our house hold?"

I sigh, "I would like to see Vera, or Elliot, it doesn't matter."

He scratches his chin, "Well, Miss Vera is here this morning so maybe you can talk to her. Miss Vera, a visitor!" Victor announces and walks away, saying, "I will go get the fresh bread and some water as you two talk." He proceeds to the kitchen.

Vera walks down the stairs and pauses half way when she sees me, "Why are *you* here?" she says in a snooty voice. I groan, "Not today Vera, I want to ask you about your mother. I think you have heard my brother also has Dragon Cough."

"So?"

"Well, our family only saw Dr. Misher and he has no hope to give us. Your family must have seen many doctors, so maybe one of the experts has a cure? Please, I am desperate!"

"Oh, so you think I actually have a cure and I am just letting people drop dead like they are cattle? That would make my dad a great mayor!" she says sarcastically.

"No, but, are you saying no one has a cure?" I reply my hopes dropping.

"Yeah, haven't you been listening, all of the doctors said that my Mummy has no hope, except..." Vera says looking upstairs.

"What?"

"Nothing", Vera dismisses.

"I want to know!"

"Well..." Vera looks down at her feet.

"Yes? Come on, anything? What?" I plead.

"My stupid brother Elliot thinks that he knows where a cure can be found, but it's ridiculous." Her voice trails off, she looks very sad and her arrogant face softens.

"What the heck are you talking about Vera?" I snap.

She looks cross again and whines, "what's wrong with you miss temper tantrum?"

I clench my fists, "does he have a cure, or not?"

"Well, Elliot reads a lot in school, like he brings home a pile as tall as he is to read. One of the scholars at his school mentioned a crazy scientist who lives out beyond the dark forest. Supposedly this guy once visited the school and bragged about all kinds of crazy stuff. Like magic curing potions, making servants out of clay, indoor toilets and other such nonsense. The man sounds like a raving freak." "Fine, fine, I get it, completely bonkers…but tell me where your brother is now! I have lots of questions for him", I say earnestly.

9 ELLIOT AT SCHOOL

I walk up to a large sign that says "the Volozhin Yeshiva". It is a one-story schoolhouse building with a large roof that is covered with black slate shingles. The walls are pearly white and have six windows on the side I can see. There is a little spot surrounded by rocks that is green and grassy, and there are stone platforms leading to the top. There is a chimney on the top that is puffing out a little smoke. I walk up the main path to the school and open the black wooden door. My eyes adjust to the dimmer indoor light. I can see about ten rows of small light wooden desks, with about five desks in each row. In every wooden desk is a student. All the boys are wearing black kippas on their heads and are wearing dark clothing with white shirts. At the front of the room there is a big chalkboard filled with writing in Russian and in Hebrew. A very old man is in the front of the room with almost no hair and a black kippa balanced on the top of his shiny head. He has a mean look to his face as his dark brown eyes look straight at me. I know who he is, Akiva Eiger. He has come to my house once or twice with Father talking about the laws in the Torah. Father said Akiva wants to retire but there is no one to replace him. I tap gently on the archway that leads into the classroom. Every one turns to look as the teacher stops talking. I lift my head and say, "Elliot Hingleffer, I need to speak with you, stat!"

The teacher says firmly, "You are disturbing our class young lady! can you not see this? Maybe this conversation could wait until after class?" He says in a question that was more of an order.

I repeat firmly, "Elliot has to see me now, it is about his mother!"

Elliot stands up and says, "My Mom, is she okay?" Elliot is a blond haired boy with pudgy cheeks and soft blue eyes. His shoulders are broad and his hands are smooth looking with no calluses. He is a bit chubby, and he is wearing a white shirt and black pants like the other boys.

I say, "I need to talk with you, outside, now! Move it Elliot! Can't you see that you are disturbing the class?"

He quickly moves from behind his desk and shuffles between the rows of desks to follow me out the door while clutching his schoolbooks. "I don't think I even know you" he calls after me.

I grab his arm, pulling him out of the classroom, saying, "I am Natasha Weinrober!"

He looks at me blankly and then a look of recognition comes to his face and he says, "Oh, I know you! You're Vera's school friend"

I gasp, "Her school friend, never!"

He sighs, "So why do I need to speak with you, I have an exam."

I nod, "Right, I know your mother has Dragon Cough and my Brother has Dragon Cough. All the village doctors are saying there is no known cure. Vera told me that you know of a person that may know a cure to Dragon Cough"

"You dragged me out of class for this? It may not even be a real cure, so I wouldn't get my hopes up." Elliot protests.

"Please tell me anything you know, even if it is a slim

chance," I plead

Elliot sighs and continues," This scientist named Isaac Volshebnik. Well some people call him a wizard. He visited our school once and made some wild boasting about magic cures. I could say he is a bit, should I say, eccentric. He also lives way past the dark forest, so it is too much trouble to even check."

"But your Mom and my brother are sick." I am shocked at how calm he is about this.

"She will get better in no time, even if she has Dragon Cough, at least that's what everyone in my family is telling me. I hear it is not fatal. She caught it while she was cutting firewood in the snow. I wanted to cut the firewood but she told me to study for this exam, which I am missing by the way if you don't let me get back in there."

"Well, guess what, she has Dragon Cough and they are lying to you! Dragon Cough is almost always fatal. If you and I don't act soon, both our family members might die," I say intensely.

"My mom won't die, she can't die!" Elliot says sputtering.

"Then help me get that cure"

"I can't, it is too far" Elliot says shaking his head no, his hands clenched at his sides.

I sigh and start to walk away. Then I turn and say, "Yeah, I am sure you're mother Svita would never go to that kind of trouble for you, if you were sick. You know what, just draw me a map to the guy's house and I will go there myself. I will try to bring back a cure for your Mom and my Brother, although honestly I don't even know the way to go. Goodbye Elliot, it was nice meeting you. "

I start to walk away when I hear him cry after me. "Wait! I can probably find a map at the school."

I pause and look back at him. He looks conflicted and

then seems to make up his mind.

"Look, just for your safety, maybe you should travel with me, okay? A little girl cannot make a trip like this alone, that's insane! I will lead you to that place around the dark forest. " he says slowly.

I am glad he has changed his mind, but angry about the tone of his comments, "And what's wrong with women? We women can be as strong as men! And by the way, if we are going to do this in time, then we don't go 'around' the dark forest, no we have to go 'straight through' the dark forest."

That took Elliot aback, "No one has ever gone through the dark forest for as long as anyone can remember. It's just not done. I know the best route to travel little girl."

I look at him with displeasure, the week's frustrations have built up in me, and so I reach out and grip his arm firmly and gave him a shove. "Wake up Elliot, we don't have time! The seconds, minutes and days are burning! This is not a nature hike we need to go on."

Shocked, he looks at me with amazement, "How dare you! I'm the son of the town mayor!"

I look at him with a stern look. "I'm not asking your permission. Help me or get out of my way."

Elliot starts to say something and hesitates. "Well, I still don't know, I mean…. Fine! We can go your way unless it looks very dangerous"

I relax and am glad to get agreement. I'm surprised in myself for my resolve, but I keep going. "Done. You go get the provisions and the map you mentioned to find this guy. I can get us horses to ride. We leave at dawn. Meet me by the end of the village road."

He looks shocked, "Wait, are we going to tell our parents?"

I shake my head, "No, if we do they will probably just

say no -and we can never get the cure and then my brother and your mom will die!"

He agrees weakly, "Ok, see you at dawn. I might as well take the rest of this exam. Hard to believe an exam was all I had to dread prior to our talk"

I put both thumbs up and walk away.

.

10 LEAVING NIKUDA

I silently go downstairs and into the kitchen. The snow is drifting onto our window leaving a beautiful pattern. I hear my parents walk downstairs and into the sitting room. They are arguing about something.

I walk in, " is everything alright?"

They look at me funny, "no, well yes… were fine."

My voice cracks, "will Alexey be okay?" I ask, already knowing the answer.

They shake their heads as my mother speak "Sweetest, we don't know. We hoped that Dr. Misher could tell us a cure, but all we have now is to pray."

She breaks into tears, flowing freely down her face.

I run to my room and sit on the bed. I feel so upset that I throw a book across the room. I know crying isn't going to solve the problem, but one thing can, to get my brother aid before time runs out.

Can I really do this? Is this just craziness and desperation? I truly do not know but I know doing nothing is unbearable.

I wait until the house is dark and everyone is sleeping. I start packing a bag. What do you pack when you don't know how long you will be gone and what your going to run into? I grab a leather satchel bag and put my torah study book, two shirts, extra pants and underwear, a few packets of food, toothbrush, tinder and flint, a half loaf of bread and my water canteen. I peek into Alexey's room one more time and whisper, "don't worry, I will come back. I will find a cure for you."

It is time for me to slip out while everyone is asleep.

I throw my bag over my shoulder and creep out in my socks, so my heavy boots will not make noise. I slip on my boots at the door, and then slowly open the front door. I breathe in the cold night air and take my first step into my adventure.

Something is pulling on my coat as I keep walking out the door, when I turn around, Yacov, my dog, is following me.

"Yacov, go home, you aren't needed where I'm going!" I whisper loudly.

He whimpers. I knew if I try to leave without him he will start to bark loudly.

I sigh, "fine but don't eat so much, ok, I'm limited!"

He ruffs in a sign of understanding, jumping up and down on me as I walk away from the house. I walk past the big red barn, the animals all asleep inside. The barn is a big dark silhouette against a sky full of stars above.

I walk out our front gate and follow the village main road for a few miles. It is slow going, as there is only a half moon above to light my way. I have to avoid ruts in the road. I can hear an owl hooting and the rustle of several small animals in the undergrowth next to the village road. I pass silently by several of our neighbor's small houses, which are all dark. It's very silent and still as I keep trudging down the road with my pack. The sky is starting to brighten ahead of me as dawn approaches. I want to find a place where I can rent a donkey or horse for the journey and I increase my pace, hoping to arrive just after dawn.

Finally, coming around a corner of the road, I can see a sign that reads, 'small donkeys to tall horses for lease or purchase'. I walk to the door and carefully knock. Hopefully this was not too early, since most of the villagers wake early to do chores at sunup.

A tall man with a curly grey beard walks out. He is wearing a checkered blue shirt and overalls. He looks annoyed to be disturbed and quickly barks out. "And what do you want rascally child?"

I speak up, "I need a horse or donkey to rent, sir."

He looks at me skeptically, "and what would you need this animal for?"

I stare straight into his eyes; "I need it to help me go through the dark forest and beyond to the far village."

"You mean to go around the dark forest, right? No one goes through that wretched forest."

"No, I meant what I said."

The man laughs mirthlessly, showing his tea-stained teeth.

"You know how dangerous it is in the forest, mmm, you do not know what you're putting yourself into."

I shake my head; "I am going the fast way so I can save my brother in time."

The man frowns, "you are a brave little child I must say, but I cannot give you a donkey or horse if you have no money and certainly not to risk my property in the dark forest on some crazy adventure."

I think about it, "Sir what is your name?"

"Marc, Marc Anosov."

I remember that name; "Mr. Anosov, you and your wife would rent my father a donkey every time he went to the neighboring synagogues or traveling. He said you were both sweet and hospitable, always ready to lend a horse to one in need." I was about to say more when I stop, seeing anger welling up in him

"Fine! Maybe when my wife was here, but she is gone now and is never coming back."

I am shocked. "I...I'm so sorry, I didn't realize"

He shouts, "Leave me be! Find another farm, but not mine!" he shuts the door with a hard thud.

I stand on the edge of his porch, stunned, looking at the door that had just slammed. The shock wears off and is replaced by a strong wave of panic. This is not going how I expected. I force myself to calm down. It is not that far to the forest edge and I likely would have had to walk the donkey most of the way through the thick forest regardless, so maybe this is for the better. I doubt I have enough supplies to feed an animal the whole way and back anyway.

I leave Anosov's farm and continue my way along the old village trail. The trail is overgrown and sometimes hard to follow. The pine trees press into the trail on both sides, making it dark and gloomy. It is slow going.

I walk a little further until I am facing the edge of the Village of Nikuda. This is it. This is when I truly have to start my journey.

11 THROUGH THE DARK FOREST

I stand at the end of the village path and wait for Elliot. Yacov looks back towards the village and barks. I pat his shoulder reassuringly and turn around. I look eastward towards the edge of the dark forest. Yacov whimpers.

I chuckle "Its okay, I bet not all the horrible stories are true about the forest."

He whimpers again.

I laugh, "Now you're just being silly."

It is an hour past our designated meeting time. I wonder if Elliot chickened out or told his parents and they grounded him. I wonder if I should keep going without a map. Did Elliot tell his parents and then they told my parents? What a mess. If I went back to get a map from the school, my parents might be there and forbid me to go on such a dangerous trip. I should have expected such trouble from Vera's brother.

As I am thinking about what to do next, I hear someone approaching. The voice is singing, but I could not make out the words. Coming around the bend I see Elliot wearing a navy blue cloak.

"What took you so long, did you stop to have tea and chocolate pastries?" I ask.

"If you must know, packing for a long trip takes awhile. The packing made me tired, so I had to add some more fuel." Elliot says tapping his belly.

I laugh; the boy is indeed a softie! Oh well, it will be okay to have the company along.

We proceed to walk and Elliot ends up requesting we stop every twenty minutes or so to have a 'break' from walking and a start on eating. In his bag is about one hundred different choices of meals, beef salted, buttered crackers, chocolate ruglagh, chocolate babka, chicken soup, halvah, boiled eggs, pickles, mashed potato's, two thick loaves of bread, a box of raspberry filled chocolate, and more. I am amazed to see such luxury in his overstuffed backpack. Did he eat like this every day? If I did, I would not fit out my cottage door.

I am not going to complain as long as he is carrying the load.

"Here, let me show you the map that I got from Teacher," he says, munching between words, "I think it leads to that wizard's tower!"

I look at him funny, "wizard's tower? That sounds like something out of a kid's fairy tale Elliot!"

Saying it out loud makes me realize how silly this whole adventure sounds. I have left home and journeyed into the deep forest hoping this will lead to a great doctor, not to this fairy tale myth.

He shrugs, "When you have no other options, crazy might be the way to go."

I chuckle, "you think he's going to help us? I asked

around about that guy, heard the last time that wizard guy came to our village, people felt he was pretty flakey!"

He shakes his head in disagreement "I can't believe it, you wiping off a possibility like that! You talked me into this trip! I should have stayed home."

"Yes, run home Elliot. You can sit in your soft home not caring about the people around you, about even a neighbor until you are the person in need."

Elliot looks hurt. I feel bad; there is my temper again. "I didn't actually mean it, I just got a little angry. I'm just so desperate to help Alexey and it all seems so hopeless. I don't know if I'm going on this trip cause I really believe it might work or just to get away."

He is silent a moment, then looks at me openly not knowing what to say.

I wave my hand, and say reassuringly, "Ok, enough with the puppy eyes! We will go to this 'wizard'! Happy?"

He smiles, "Ok, I'm happy you see sense in this path, now, off to the wizard!"

As we keep our pace, I finally tell him we can't have so many rest 'breaks', he sadly nods and keeps moving.

As we walk further into the dark forest, my sense of dread diminishes. This isn't as bad as I thought it would be.

Elliot holds up the map and points to a town called Sakher, "This is the best place to buy pastries, and oh look! St Petersburg! Wait you know what St Petersburg is, even though you have never been there. I have been there many times, my father, the mayor, takes me. And look here, Flishbec the best area for inns.

I roll my eyes, "Ok, I get it, you have gone every where!"

He snickers, "That's not true I haven't gone here. He pointed to the corner of the map that was an Island. "It says Buyan Island"

"I know that place! I read about the legend in a book! It comes and goes every 100 years!"

Elliot grins and says, "I want to go there someday. It sounds so interesting. Imagine the people there, always unhinged from time every hundred years."

"But why would you want to be gone for one hundred years, your family would miss you" I ask surprised.

"Not my dad." He says dejectedly.

"Why not?" I say curious of the answer.

"Everything I do has to be better than I actually did," he admits.

"What if you do not do so good?" I ask hesitantly.

Elliot shudders, "Then he would have a temper. My father thought your brother Alexey was the perfect child; he would always be the top of every class. My grades come hard to me, but I don't think your brother had to study that much. He was effortlessly brilliant. My father thought I should be more like him, until he left the school."

I can see that Elliot is uncomfortable with this conversation so I change to a new topic.

"Tell me more about what your teacher said about this wizard guy?" I ask.

He smiles. "The man's name is Isaac Volshebnik. He was said to be one of the greatest scientist of all time, he could heal, fix, and make almost anything. But when the Czar wanted to control him and have him move to St.Petersburg he just disappeared."

I shake my head. "I see why you would want to see him, so that he could give us a serum to cure our family members."

He nods, "Yes, and this map shows us where he lives."

Yacov yelps and chews on Elliot's cloak. "Hey stop it you mutt, this cloak is velvet and hand embroidered wool!"

I laugh, "Why are you even wearing a cloak?"

He looks at me like I should know; "I have a cloak so I stay warm." He smirks, "where's your cloak?"

I roll my eyes, "I didn't forget one because I don't own one, plus I brought my jacket. Your cloak is soft, but this is waterproof. Let's see which one is more useful."

We continue to walk until Elliot starts to complain that his feet hurt, "Fine, we will stop and rest for the night.

12 CAMPING IN THE DARK FOREST

We walk through a thicker area of the forest. It feels like the forest itself is pushing back on us. The sun has set below the tree line, making the dark woods even darker. My legs feel sore and I can tell Elliot is tired. We finally come across a clearing in the forest, sort of like a meadow. This looks like a good place to make camp for the night.

We sit down on a nice flat patch of dirt and I get a little bit of wood, flint, and a rock and start to make a fire. Elliot on the other hand took out a small pillow and sits down on it.

"Elliot, tell me a little about yourself other than the fact that you're snobby and uptight"

He thinks about that question. "Well, I don't even know where to start...I was born in October, a bright blue eyed baby. I was one and a half when I started talking and lost my first tooth when I was six years old."

I laugh, "That's some accomplishment!"

He sneers, "Well, I had my bar mitzvah a few months ago."

"That's such an accomplishment, knowing you are the one of thousands who celebrate their bat/bar mitzvah!"

"Well I read a lot and I study for exams. That's been my life so far." He says with a sigh. "But someday I want to be a mayor like my Daddy."

"Does reading a lot of books prepare you to be mayor of Nikuda?"

"Uhm…I don't know" Elliot stammers, "what about you? You can't be a rabbi like your Daddy."

That gets me angry. "Who says I can't be a rabbi? I can be anything I want to be. Maybe I want to be like Dr. Misher."

"You want to marry Dr. Misher? He's kind of old for you." Elliot says, not understanding.

"NO!" I face palm my forehead. "Not marry Dr. Misher, BE a doctor like him!! Why is that so hard to understand?"

"Oh ok, that's a first." Elliot says skeptically, trying to calm me down.

We each setup a camp tent with sticks to brace the canvas. I remember how Alexey had shown me how to do this.

Somehow his version had come out looking more like a tent, where as mine looked messier with the supports at odd angles. It will not be comfortable but it will have to do. Elliot has packed an actual army style one-person tent. He seems to have a lot of trouble figuring out how to set it up, but after awhile it comes into shape.

While Elliot works on his tent, I make a campfire from some scattered wood I found. We eat some of the provisions Elliot has brought. It was probably worth having him along just for the wonderful food he brought, most of which I had only seen through shop windows.

Elliot tells me he is tired and goes into his camp tent. I

start to add more firewood, when Elliot complains, "Natasha, the ground is really hard!"

I answer him, "Welcome to Earth, where did you think we would stay?"

He shrugs, "I thought we were going to stay at an inn. The last inn I went to with my father gave us these blueberry biscuits glazed in caramel gouache."

I smirk, "Ok, were not going to run into a lot of Inn's in the dark forest. And inn's cost money, how would we pay?"

He steps out of his tent and looks at me like I forgot something, "I brought a big bag of rubles, and I told my mother that in my note."

"Your what?"

"I wrote a note to my mom telling her where and why I was going."

"That was probably what I should have done." I say quietly, suddenly feeling bad.

"You forgot to write a note?" he asks astonished; "Now your parents probably think you're kidnapped or dead!"

I agree, not having thought of that before. Now I'm worried I have added to my parent's grief. How stupid of me. Why didn't I think of this before? Maybe they would hear about Elliot's note and assume I had gone with him. Or they would assume I had disappeared and been killed like poor Katya. This was terrible.

"Thanks Elliot for giving me one more thing to feel bad about", I say angrily.

I climb into my tent to try to get some sleep.

I'm woken by the faint sound of a voice. Am I dreaming it or is it a real voice, like a discordant song in the distance. I climb out of my tent and look around. The sun is just cresting the horizon, lighting everything up a fire red color. I go over shake Elliot's tent.

"Elliot! Wake up, I hear something!" There is no answer.

Alarmed, I open the flap of his tent. There is no one there except his pile of blankets. His cloak and boots are missing. That idiot! Where did he go?

I climb out and see his shoe prints leading further into the woods, following chicken footprints. Wait a minute, why are there big chicken footprints? I follow the prints and see that it leads to a stone path. I follow the path until the trees seem to get narrower and the ground muddier. What was Elliot doing following some weird chicken trail into a swamp? Did he sneak off to go to the bathroom as far as possible from camp to be polite? Was he rustling up chicken eggs for breakfast? That thought is not entirely unwelcome. I was surprisingly getting tired of the too sweet provisions he had packed. I can't be sure if Elliot is following the chicken or the chicken is following Elliot.

Finally, much to my relief, I see Elliot ahead of me on the path, peering around some ferns.

"Elliot! There you are, I was looking all over for you!" I call out.

Elliot turns and shushes me, whispering, "Natasha, you have to see this."

I look over at where he is pointing excitedly and gasp. There, on the ground the big chicken footprints lead up to a huge pair of chicken feet with an odd house sitting on top of them.

13 BABA YAGA

The chicken feet are about the height of Elliot and they are connected to a large hut that is releasing the pungent smell of dead animals and cabbage. I step forward and ask, "Whose crazy house is this?"

He shakes his head, "I have no idea at all."

The paint is chipping off the rotting wood house, and the roof has overgrown weeds and moss on it.

"Whoevers house it is, they aren't the best housekeepers!" Elliot states, wrinkling his nose.

I nod in agreement; this person really does not understand the difference between neat and nasty. Surrounding the house are many dead trees and a swamp that is reeking in decay, which really isn't helping my nose. There is a lot of garbage, old shoes, rags and debris all around the hut.

I hear the sound of the voice again, very faintly, but I can't make it out. Something about the voice is almost recognizable but I can't grasp it. I knock on the round molding door, and bugs climb out and scurry around the ground.

"At least we could ask if a chicken went in here," Elliot states. "Maybe this is an inn?"

"Seriously?" I ask.

I stand next to him, and knock harder.

A few moments later the door creaks open slowly, we both step back in surprise as the door swings open, and a horror meet our eyes. An old woman opens the door. And this wasn't just any old woman; the woman has black and yellow teeth with puffy gums. She only has a few strands of grey greasy hair, and her eyeballs are raven black, pupil, iris and all. When she smiles you could see her jawbone move under her pale leathery skin, which is slightly translucent.

"Hello?" She says in a voice that sounds shrill and dissonant with an after breath that smells like mothballs. My dog, Yacov, whimpers and hides behind me as I stand with my head up. "Yacov, get behind that old tire" I say loudly, pointing. My dog hops behind the old tire without hesitating, spooked.

"Well, little children, I want to know who you are and why you are on my front porch!" The old woman asks with a half smile.

I am about to answer and beat a hasty retreat, when I distinctly heard Katya's voice call out from inside the house.

"Natasha? Can that be your voice?! Help! Help!"

I nudge Elliot urgently, "did you hear that?" I whisper at him.

He looks at me funny, "hear what?"

"That voice, it sounded like my friend Katya's!"

He still has the same skeptical face, "Who is Katya?"

"Don't you know? Katya's my friend that comes during the holidays."

"Oh! She's the girl that plays with you and Vera!"

"Again, we were not playing with Vera, we were fighting!"

He shrugs, "Whatever you say" and turns back to the old woman to ask, "Who are you?"

"Just an old mostly harmless woman" She mumbles with a toothy grin, "You better come inside, I sense you are in grave danger young ones."

I interrupt her, "I want to know about that voice I heard, it sounded like a friend of mine from inside" I insist.

"Yes, you better come look quickly" she motions me inside with her withered hand.

Elliot grabs my arm, "Are you nuts? What do you think your doing?"

I free my arm from his grip, "I heard my friend's voice and I'm going to find her! I'm not afraid of some old woman."

He pleads, "Well, I'm not going in there, no matter what! This whole thing is really creepy"

I push him back, "So your telling me your staying in the dark woods alone all by yourself? You're saying you are a coward?"

He looks around him hesitantly, "Curse this dark forest! No, I don't like the idea of being alone in this creepy place. Splitting up is certainly a bad idea so I better come to protect you".

Great, how does he always turn things around so I'm the helpless one?

When we walk in through the low doorway, I can feel the air thicken and the lights grow dim. The walls are covered in animal skins of all sorts. The dining table is cluttered with jars of marbles, packages, boxes and other artifacts. Every where you turn there were always piles of stuff, jars, a blue one here, a red one here, a black one there, each one was filled with all sorts of floating things like pickles, buttons, matches, and more. It was dizzying to take in. The hallway was full of boxes like the lady just moved, there were so many sizes, small, large, medium and in between.

Then, I see table that has a pretty chessboard, one of the only uncluttered areas of the piles of mess. I looked at it closely and see that they are so finely carved that they look like real tiny people. I touch one and I feel so sad for some reason, "That is my collection, I have been making this chessboard for a very, very long time."

The old woman said behind me, her hand suddenly lighting upon my shoulder, which gives me a shiver.

I drew back and asked, "How long did it take?"

"A few centuries give or take!" she shrugs.

I laugh nervously, "that's...why that's impossible, who do you think you are?"

She replies, "Who do I think I am? Who do I know I am! I am BABA YAGA!" She says with a low bow and flourish.

Then she turns around to us.

"I was alone wishing for a young child like you two to show up, and it came true when a little girl named Katya came to my area of the forest at the perfect moment! Oh I waited such a long time. It made me feel like a spider. Aren't spiders lovely little things? So patient and they make such delicate little traps"

My jaw drops, "You...you have Katya right now?"

She nods with some glee.

"Is she safe, is she unhurt?" I ask with a shaky voice.

" She is mostly... unharmed, Is she safe, well...how safe do you feel?"

I shudder, feeling insecure.

"Now, young children, time for my dinner, your pretty, pretty memories." Elliot starts to whimper and curl into a ball, so I said, "I will offer my memories! Leave Elliot alone"

Baba Yaga looks at me funny "How noble...you want to have happy memories sucked out of you?"

I nod, not seeing any option, and sat in a chair. Before she touches my head I state, "No stories my babushka told me about you says that you feed on happy memories"

She smiles broadly, "People talk about me...I am that popular?"

I shudder "No you haunt children's nightmares."

She shrugs, "Almost the same thing" and caresses my head.

I could see before my eyes what she was taking away. There I was about a year ago playing with Yacov under the beautiful azure sky, the weather was warm and Alexey was playing with David who was only one year old at the time. I was playing with a faded red ball on the side of the road during taxing day.

"Ah, Yes! This is a nice memory" Baba Yaga murmurs, but things were about to change. I had not been watching where my ball was going so it rolled into the pathway. I bent over and touched my ball when I felt a thud on my back. I turned around and Captain Vladislav, one of the Czar's soldiers, was picking himself up and glaring at me. "Are you ok sir?" I asked politely. I had accidently knocked him over.

He snarled, "you stupid girl, you made me trip!" he said, walking up to me.

"I didn't see you sir," I blurted out.

He spat on the floor, "Maybe you should look up once a while!" and took me by the arm, twisting it and threw me to the ground. "Maybe you can see your ball now!" With a growl, he got out his rifle and brought it to aim at my heart.

Alexey suddenly stood in front of him. "Is there a

problem sir?" he asked innocently.

The solider nodded, "This idiot of a kid tripped me and made me fall over!" Alexey still standing in the way said, "this is my fault, I should have been watching her...why don't we forgive, forget, and move on, eh?"
The soldier snarled, "in your dreams!" and started beating up my brother violently, hitting him with the butt of the rifle. I heard myself screaming again in my mind. Before the memory was over, Baba Yaga reeled back, "Worthless child, your memories are too bittersweet! Bah! If you are not food for my mind, I will roast you all for dinner to feed my stomach!" She yells, storming off to her kitchen.

14 ESCAPE FROM BABA YAGA

I was still dizzy from the memory draining Baba Yaga had done and too shook up to make a run for it. What was she going to get out of the kitchen to finish us off with? A rifle? A magic wand of death? Did it matter which one?

Elliot cried out to Baba Yaga before she left the room, "Wait! Let me ask you one question!"

She waves her hand about in a flutter, "Why should I bother?"

"Because..." Elliot said casting his gaze around the room, until it lit upon the ornate chess set. "Because... its about chess!"

She turns around suddenly. "About chess you say? Well that does sound interesting!"

"I like chess" Elliot states weakly.

Baba Yaga laughs loudly "I'll give you a go then, if you win everyone can go free. If you lose, then you my handsome boy are going to complete my chess set and fill in the place of my missing knight...forever frozen as a chess piece!" She laughs maniacally.

Elliot gulps and slowly nods.

I step forward, "If Katya is alive, bring her out! She goes free also with us when Elliot wins. Everyone goes free, right?"

"When he wins? You mean if he wins, and that's a pretty small chance, isn't it girl? I have been playing chess since the game was invented."

She thought a moment, paused, groaned, and said, "Fine! I like the extra drama of your friend's life also in the balance. You think your ready for upping the wager, boy?"

"I should let you know, I am the best chess player in my class at Yeshiva school." Elliot says uncertainly, "well, I mean out of the 30 of us."

"I'm shaking boychik" Baba Yaga cackles.

Baba Yaga leans over in her chair and with the end of her walking stick traces a rough square on the dirty wooden floor. The stick leaves a chalky greasy trail and the area of the floor turned strangely fluid. Like a drain emptying the fluid seeps down leaving a half-meter dark pit in the floor. I gasp.

A shaky hand reaches out of the pit, clawing at the edge. Then a familiar head of reddish hair pokes out and grasped her way out of the pit to collapse onto the wooden floor next to the pit. The hole quickly closes up with a pop sound, as if it was never there.

Katya gasps for air and looks around wildly. "Oh my god, its you! It is really you Natasha! Am I? Am I dead? Am I out of that awful pit and in heaven now?" She asked bewildered, her eyes blinking.

"Heaven? Well I did tidy up a bit, because I just knew company was coming, but this is far from heaven girlie" Baba Yaga says laughing maniacally.

Upon hearing the voice she sighs, not wanting to turn around to face Baba Yaga. "Oh no! Natasha, are you captured too trying to save me?"

I shake my head defiantly, "no, we are all leaving right after a quick chess game, right Elliot?"

Elliot nods, "Yes, quick, very quick!"

Elliot sits down gingerly in front of her and we gather round. I try to angle around behind Baba Yaga, to perhaps strike her while she is focused on the chess set.

"Hey girlie, back over next to your friend, old Baba Yaga has eyes in the back of her head...literally." Grossed out, I quickly sit close to Elliot.

Elliot looks over the chessboard. "Who gets the side with the missing knight?"

She cackles, "You actually thought you were getting the full side, you're funny"

The chess game starts. Elliot, his hand shaking a bit, moves his pawn forward two spaces. Instantly, the old witch pushes forward her pawn two spaces. Elliot moves his knight to F3 and Baba Yaga quickly counters with Nf6. I'm so nervous, I don't want to watch.

The game proceeds until I can tell that Baba Yaga is winning, Elliot is down three pieces, technically four because he already started with a missing knight. Baba Yaga turns her head up to Elliot, "so, this is hard, no?" she probes sadistically.

Elliot nods, "I never thought that I would be so close to death by a chess game" She cackles, "neither did any of these others who became my pieces."

Elliot moves his queen to G6, which I think is a mistake because Baba Yaga's knight takes his queen. She laughs and slaps the queen onto the floor. I pick it up and caress it in my hands. "That is pretty rough treatment for a piece that was once a person, or if it really is still sort of a person."

I study the piece in my hand, the carving of the queen is so detailed, the face proud and sad at the same time. The hair is painted gold with brown streaks, and the eyes have a look of melancholy.

I whisper to it, in a voice tinged with pity, "You must have been a person with hopes and dreams, with plans for the future. How long have you been a chess piece? Ten years? Twenty? One hundred?"

I hear a faint whisper, "too long to even remember"

I look around the room, "who just spoke?"

Baba Yaga snaps at me, "don't interrupt child, I am about to win!" and turns away.

I realize it was the chess piece in my hand that spoke, if that is even possible. I lift it closer to my ear and it speaks again,

"I think your friend needs some help, he is losing, and I should know. I have been playing chess for three hundred years."

I whisper, "Could you help us win the game?"

"Why should I?" the piece says coldly.

"Don't you want to be human again?" I plead.

"I don't really remember being human, I only remember being a chess piece." The queen says flatly.

"So your saying, you would want to be pushed around against your own will- just because someone is playing on the white side?"

She pauses for a second, "I never thought of it like that. However, I am a queen. I am so very important, next to the king of course. When your friend loses there will be a full set for us, then our side won't lose all the time. Isn't winning better than being human?"

I shrug, "do you know what I did today?"

"No, what?"

"I snuck an extra piece of babka from Elliot's bag. Do you know what babka is? Well, this kind was dark chocolate with a hint of cinnamon and vanilla, and it was so good."

She sighs, "I remember I was going to the market to get some bread when a strange chicken footed hut came rambling in my way."

I nod, "Do you remember what it feels like when your waking up to the sound of birds chirping and the sun rising? Do you remember coming inside from the bitter cold and propping yourself up near the dancing fire?"

She looks up at me. I continue, seeing she is listening intently, "I always do my chores everyday until Sabbath, the time of rest, where our family gathers together at the dinner table eating challah and chicken soup, then ending the day with a time where just me and my brothers would snuggle up together near the fire until it died out. Then I would wake up again and start the week new."

"Oh my child, you reminded me of everything that I have lost, I will do anything in your favor."

"Good, help my friend with some of your expert chess advice."

I walk up to Elliot and whisper in his ear, "don't freak- just trust me and listen to the voice from this chess piece". I quickly slip the chess piece into his shirt collar.

He looks at me funny, and then looks startled, as I hear some buzzing from the chess piece whispering to his ear. Then he begins to grin, but faces Baba Yaga and covers his smile with his hand.

Baba Yaga smiles, "I am ahead a knight, queen, rook, and five pawns.

Elliot grins and moves his piece with a determined thud on the board, "but you also are in checkmate now!"

Baba Yaga jumps up and runs around the board looking at it from several different angles, "How! How is this possible!"

Elliot replies calmly, "I told you, I'm the best in my Yashiva school!"

She calms down slightly after some time, "all right, FINE! Your friends can go as I promised."

I shake my head, "You said 'everyone', that means the chess pieces too."

She fumes, "NO!! That set took me three hundred years to build!"

I look at her seriously, "We had a deal. We had a wager. You said 'Everyone' could go free. Maybe honoring your bets doesn't mean anything to you."

She has smoke coming out of her ears, "Argh! I always honor a bet. But we are having a rematch!" and she waves her scrawny arm and everyone is suddenly thrown out of the hut as if by a powerful foul smelling wind, even the chess pieces, which magically turn back into confused people as they hit the ground.

The queen chess piece woman walks towards me, "thank you young child, you did so much for us." She says with a formal bow.

I wave my hand as she and the other chess piece people walk away and said,"zay gusent!!" and turn to Elliot and Katya and say, "Let's get moving before she demand a rematch!"

"Natasha! You saved my life! I can't believe it! I don't know what to say!" Katya stammers, tears welling up in her eyes.

Eliot coughs, "I um, believe I helped,"

She rolls her eyes and runs over to hug me. I hug her tightly and smile, but of course Elliot has to ruin the moment and jump into the group hug.

I quickly push him away and say, "You ruin everything you know"

He smiles and says, "I know"

Yacov is still waiting outside and has not wandered far. He is overjoyed to see us and hops up and down barking.

"What a good doggy!" Katya says delighted.

We find where some of our supplies landed and salvage what we can. Katya finds her hunting bow and quiver of arrows.

Elliot sees this and says, "Whoa! A bow and arrow! Maybe I better carry that in case of danger!"

I ask skeptically, "Are you at all a good shot with that Elliot?"

Elliot hesitates. "I've read several books on archery actually".

I laugh, "Yeah, that's what I thought. Katya is a crack shot with a bow".

Elliot is impressed, "How do you get these skills Katya?"

"That's easy Elliot, just be raised as the only child of a father who really wanted a son and not a daughter!"

We go back to the forest path and keep following the path several hours, until we are tired. I'm glad to put some distance between that weird area and us.

We continue to walk and Katya surveys the unfamiliar trail and asks me where we are going,

"Well, we are going to the Wizard", Elliot replies.

She tilts her head, "the wizard?" and looks at me questioningly.

I answer, "He's a scientist who live fairly far away. We have to take a short cut through the deep forest so that we can come back quickly."

"Why do you want to go to this 'wizard' scientist guy anyway?"

I sigh, "Yeah, you missed a lot while you were gone. We are going because Elliot's Mom Svita and my Brother Alexey are sick with Dragon Cough."

Katya nods, "Well, maybe you can bring me back to my home and then you two go on your little quest."

 Elliot snaps, "we already passed your home on the way here, so you can walk back yourself if you want to."

She shook her head quickly, not wanting to be alone in the dark forest.

I sigh, "If you come with us you will have a higher chance of not running into Baba Yaga again"

Katya walks closer to me, "but what if we run into something even more hideous then her?"

 I shrug, "how can something be worse than Baba Yaga? She's hideous from skin to bone!"

She shrugs, "I still think it would be smart to go together to my house."

I shake my head sadly; " We have to get the serum as quick as possible. Every hour, every day matters. Then we can get you home."

She sighs, "Ok, I'll come, but only if you stay right by my side"

I laugh, "of course I will, you can count on me!"

She smiles, "right, I never doubted you. I feel safe if you're here to protect me Natasha"

Elliot pipes up, "Katya, don't forget that I am here also"

Katya thought about this and said, "Yes Elliot, don't worry! I'm sure Natasha can protect you also.

And we proceed on our way down the forest path

15 THE VILLAGE OF SAKHER

Finally we make it out of the Dark Forest without any more trouble. It was good to be through the thick trees and onto a real road again. I feel like I can breathe easier.

Elliot insists on celebrating by staying a night in a comfy inn. He blabs on and on about the village of Sakher we are heading towards. "It has an amazing inn, the beds are almost as soft as mine, and every morning they give you warm buttered scones."

But, when the woods part we see that the town looks deserted, and all the doors are barred and locked. The shops are all closed. I grunt, "how hospitable" and proceed to walk forward.

Katya grimaces, "what if this village is actually filled with a bunch of trolls that have already ate the town up?

I pat Katya on the head, "What did Baba Yaga do to this little brain up here?"

"I don't know, but I still think it is possible. We should be super cautious."

We continue to walk in the rain down a dusty dirt road and end up in front of the village hall. All the houses are locked up. The ground is a muddy grey brown because all the topsoil has washed away. Which reminds me that it is so rainy here, the rain just keeps coming like a never-ending saltshaker. We see a door that has a weathered sign saying, 'Sven's Inn'. We walk in and see that the place is deserted, except for a short man with a dark grey beard and light blue eyes. He sees us enter and is so surprised he almost drops the plates he is washing.

"What are you children doing here, you should always be in your parents sight!" We look at each other and Katya says, "Oh, we are travelers."

"Travelers? So young?" He asks, his eyes wide.

"Yes, we come from Nikuda…" I say.

"My name is Sven, I run this Inn." He says.

"I am Natasha, this is Elliot and Katya, my friends" I reply.

"You should not be here," He says suddenly, looking upset.

"What? Why?" I ask cautiously. Katya starts humming out of nervousness.

"This town is very dangerous, children are going missing every day, ever since the rains fell." He says, with a wide motion of his arms upwards.

This reminds me of the rain, and how long it has been falling as we walked towards the village.

"Sir, how long exactly has it been raining?" I ask.

"Nine months. That doesn't sound very long, but try living somewhere that rains every single day. It could drive you crazy" He says gripping the table.

Elliot murmurs, "Well, this has been a gloomy year for you hasn't it."

He smiles faintly, "Now today is not bad, a light rain is good! You kind of develop a new vocabulary for different types of rain. Hard driving rain, light drizzle, heavy mist, hazy thunderstorm rain, padding hail rain, sideways rain, square rain, etc. "

"What is causing this change in the weather?" I ask curiously.

"We don't know, but I feel it will be the end of our town.

Katya interrupts me, "Enough about the rain, what are you saying about danger and how we should not be here?" She looks frightened again.

Sven looks down at the counter, "I don't want to alarm you so much, but little children are going missing. At first we thought a wolf or bear was responsible. The men of the village went on hunting parties and even ventured into the dark forest, but found nothing. We began to realize this was not the work of an animal but of things that were unnatural."

I can see Katya is getting very upset, so I try to change the topic. "Sir, may we have something to eat?"

He nods, "Yes child, broth is all I have. "

"Wait!" Elliot interrupts, "No scones? No Buttered buns?"

"The pantry flooded. I can't make baked goods with waterlogged ingredients".

Elliot looks heart broken.

He offers. "I'm glad you remember my fine baked goods from happier times."

Now Elliot looks angry. "This is unacceptable. Why did no one inform the Czar? He would have sent a group of soldiers to investigate!"

"Of course we notified the government! My bread is soft but not my head!" Sven yells, losing his temper.

"What happened?" I ask curiously.

"A group of soldiers came, led by Captain Vladislav of the Czar's royal guard. They looked all around the village, and turned it upside down searching. Then they went eastward. Several days later we received an official letter from Captain Vladislav, stating that everything was under control and the cause of the disappearances of children was found to be a family of wolves. The Captain reports that all the wolves were killed and everyone should just relax."

I shudder hearing the name of that cruel soldier who had

hurt Alexey. The report that the trouble had been dealt with did calm me however. I sensed that Sven was not assured.

"You can sleep here tonight, but please go back to your homes tomorrow. Whatever you do, don't go east. The soldiers say the trouble has been dealt with, but I don't believe it. Something stole our children from the village, one by one. Based on drag tracks, that something departs eastward. I don't believe it was a pack of wolves, as I never saw a single wolf track! I believe it is something unnatural; something wicked if you ask me! Many kids were sent away from the village to live with relatives. Many families simply just left. You should head back to where you came from if your smart."

Elliot looks at his map, drawing a finger from Sakher village, were we are at, to the Wizard tower on the map, dead east.

16 THE DOMAIN OF THE WURDLACS

We awake early the next day and pack up our bags. Sven gives us some water for the trip and wishes us luck. We hike for the entire day, in the hard driving rain. It is miserable and we are soaked, even with our rain jackets. Elliot's cloak is like a hot wet sponge on his back. He looks like he is twice as heavy with the water it has absorbed.

"Maybe we should have stayed at the Inn until it stopped raining?" Elliot ventures.

"Months of rain Elliot!" I remind him. "That's just bizarre!"

Towards dusk, as we walk in the hard pounding rain, we see another town ahead and slog through the muddy trail towards it.

Katya shivers, "Um, maybe we shouldn't go to this town."

Elliot peeres at her, letting out a sigh, "Why? Afraid of more broth?"

"What if these town people were eating all the children from that other village?"

Elliot sighs and pats Katya condescendingly on the back,

"Silly, silly Katya!"

She pushes his hand away, "Don't silly Katya me! I am serious! The man warned about east! This town is east!"

I groan, "Katya, it's raining and it's late. The place obviously must have an inn and can't possibly be a town full of evil cannibals!"

She whimpers, "Come on, let's just sleep in the forest and not risk it. So what if we are out in the rain, no one will care. Better water and discomfort than…well, you know."

I grab her hand and say, "Believe me, I am almost sure that there is no one in this village that will eat us, ok?"

She nods reluctantly.

We walk closer to the town and I notice something odd. It looks like the entire town is surrounded with something very shiny, like a soap bubble, but shinier. I walk to the edge of the forest and see it is indeed some kind of a shimmering bubble. When I touch the bubble edge my hand goes right through with a tingling feeling.

"That is so weird" I say, pulling my hand back. It is now dry from the rain.

Bravely, I step forward through the bubble edge and suddenly my clothing is dry head to toe. I motion for them to follow me.

Katya shivers, "I don't like it, it's spooky! That is what this is, its plain spooky."

Yacov walks through following me, and is about to shake the water off, but right when he turns his body he realizes there is no water on him and he barks in surprise.

Elliot jumps in and out, laughing like it was a great magic trick. He says, "Wow! Who needs a coat on, when you can just put one of these bubbles around you? I wish I had this in my home."

Katya smirks, "I am fine with a rain coat, but thanks." She reluctantly steps over the barrier.

Yacov whimpers and put his tail between his legs. I kneel over and say softly "What is it boy?"

"ROOF! ROOF!" his nose is pointing all over the place.

The ground is dry and parched, with brown remnants of plants and scattered stones. There are a few scraggly dead trees with no leaves or pine needles. The dusty road leads to the village main street. We follow the trail cautiously, not seeing any people milling about.

There are whispers all around and giggling. Out of the shadows suddenly appeared a young woman, perhaps in her early twenties. She has ice blond hair and diamond blue eyes. She is beautiful. She looks like she is kissed with gold, but, her skin is as pale as the moon. Her clothes are all white, even her shoes. She has mischief in her eyes, and it somehow captures hold of you. It makes me feel unsettled. Luckily Elliot shook me and I was okay.

I clear my throat and say, "Hello! We are wondering if there is an inn in your town? Our map said that this is the town of Wurdlac, but we had never heard of this town."

Elliot interrupts, saying, "Hey there, I am Elliot! Don't mind them, there are a lot of towns they have not seen. I, on the other hand, have gone to many places, including St. Petersburg and Moscow!"

The woman giggles, it sounds like lonely chimes. "Ah, you are quite the traveller. I am Zmeya! Lucky for you, I own the Town's inn, so come follow me to your rest."

We walk behind her, as she is saying something about an unusual inn, but I wasn't listening since I am so busy looking around the odd town. An unusual dome shaped building caught my eye, which is about ten meters away. It seems to be aquamarine blue colored, but it was a little far away to be sure. For some reason, I am curious to go in there, but it would be impolite to ask her to just turn around and go over to the dome.

The other buildings are short and square with flat roofs. When we get to the front of Zmeya's building, Katya squeezes my hand and points up. When I looked, I noticed there is a flat roof, not a triangular slanted roof, like I am used to back home. It seems most of the houses here are of this design. I thought of how impractical it is to have a flat roof. I wondered if they have to constantly shovel snow off the roof in our heavy Russian winters. But I remember there is that strange bubble that keeps out the rain, so it must keep out snow too. It seems to keep things warm too, because all the people here are lightly dressed. They all are thin, tall and pale like Zmeya.

I look at the outside of the door and noticed it was some shiny metal that you could see your reflection in. The woman opened the door and motions us to go inside.
We hesitate, remembering Baba Yaga's house. She smiles that cold beautiful smile again and says, "Children, please, do I look like some kind of a monster?"
Elliot quickly straightens his hair up and says, "Lets go inside, she seems nice, right?"
I sigh; I can tell that he likes her. She asks, "Where are you from strangers?"
I answer slowly, "Nikuda, so is Elliot."
Her eyes brighten, "I used to live in Nikuda! Why, it seems like decades ago since I have been there! We must talk of those old times inside and have a meal."
We step inside. It is so bright inside that it hurts my eyes. I have to half-close my eyes and squint. I look around and all around me are reflections on the shiny walls! My reflection bounced onwards above me, below me, and beside me. It is dizzying.
"You sure like mirrors in this place!" Katya observes.
The woman laughs that odd chime like laugh again. "Yes, it

is, because then I can see my face every time I wake up". She has the voice of cats purring. It is soft and slightly creepy and makes you want to run, but when you look at her pretty face then you think it is a melody coming out of her mouth. I feel trapped by her voice again with no one to nudge me, because I can see that her voice and eyes have trapped them too. She commands us to follow her and we do, for we have no control of our feet. It feels like we are floating along behind her in a dream. We pass through an archway to the next large house.

Similar to Zmeya's house, this also has mirrors on all sides. It is filled with more beautiful blond and diamond blue-eyed people. There are not only women, but also men. The men have grey clothes on. The women also all wear bright white outfits. I suspected perhaps this is a meal place, with dishes and wine and silverware all around the big central table. I was a bit perplexed, for where is the food in this dining hall? Maybe it is still cooking, although it if is like food back home I would surely have smelled it.

I sit down next to Zmeya, Elliot quickly makes sure to sit closely on the other side of her. Katya carefully sits at the end of the long table. I saw she is still clutching her bow tightly and seems to have one hand hovering above her quiver. She does not trust the Wurdlacs and I'm starting to get a bad feeling also.

I notice then that moving around the dining hall, there are a bunch of men and women- but no children. It was a bit out of sorts, because in Nikuda, children are an important part of the village life.

I ask her, "where are all the kids"

Two of the women in white, they look pretty similar to Zmeya except one has a longer neck and has a bigger upturned nose, look at each other in questioning.

Zmeya explains, "You will have to keep your voices low,

they are all dead asleep"

I nod, sensing that they are lying in some way and that something is very, very wrong here in the Wurdlac village

17 WURDLAC BATTLE

Elliot asks, "So, I can hear my stomach rumbling, when is the food arriving?"

Zmeya says, "It's arriving! Oh look, there it is!" she points at the end of the table near where Katya is.

I look past Katya and ask, "where?"

She smiles, "Children, your so funny! But we really shouldn't play with our food, right?" and motions to the two men standing nearby.

The door opens and several more men enter. To my shock, one of them is Captain Vladislav! He looks blonder and paler than usual and his eyes are like blue diamond. Unlike the other Wurdlacs he is still dressed in his soldier's uniform with its shiny brass buttons.

"Captain Vladislav!" I shout in surprise.

He looks at me with the same cruel look as the time I had bumped him accidently, the day he had beaten Alexey so badly.

"What a small world" Captain Vladislav smirks.

"Ah, you know our dear Captain Vladislav?" Zmeya says

with a cold smile. "We made him an offer he couldn't refuse and now he is one of us!"

"You lied on that report to the government! You lied to the village of Sakher about their children!" I say shocked. "Where are the rest of the soldiers that marched to this village?"

"None of the others saw the great opportunity of joining the Wurdlacs. What a pity. I dealt with them." Captain Vladislav admitted coldly.

Zmeya looks back at me, laughing at the shock on my face. She says, "So young and so naive. Oh, you are so pretty! It would be a pity to see you die"

I snarl, "Then don't! Why are you doing this? This is insane!"

She laughs and says, "but isn't it the circle of life, you live, and then, you die!" making a circle motion with her hands.

I snip, "Then why are you not dead yet?" and grab for the small camping axe tied to my bag. I lift the axe and prepare to strike her. Suddenly Captain Vladislav swiftly grabs my wrist and twists the axe from my hand. His grip is like iron. It clatters to the table in front to Zmeya.

Zmeya laughs and says, "Ah, Captain! Always so useful to have around!"

Yacov starts to nip at Vladislav's ankles, barking furiously. Captain Vladislav looks amused but with that same seething anger I've seen before, that same cruel look in his eyes. I'm holding my breath hoping he does not kill Yacov in one angry blow.

Zmeya grabs my arm in a cold and firm grip. "You are strong, young, and pretty. The reason that we have not killed you yet is because I see you have the potential to be one of us. You all could be useful to us. We are from the same village you know."

I smirk, "really? I know everyone in the village, and believe me, I would have remembered you."

She giggles, "I left that boring village of Nikuda, left my husband Marc Anosov, and left my human life behind long before you were born"

I gasp, "Wait, I know that guy, he's that old horse keeper!"

She tilts her head to one side, "He is still alive? Ah, he must be ancient, unlike myself"

I continue, "Hey, that means, you must be at least sixty!"

Elliot turns around facing her saying, "Whoa!"

She laughs, "I am one of the younger Wardlucs, Some here are over three hundred years old! The years pass, but we don't wither, we don't get disease, or die."

She takes my hand more gently and says; " now you see what it is like to be a Wurdlac, to be beautiful and young forever! How can any refuse such a gift? Join us!"

I pull my hand away, "Honestly that's very tempting, I mean the living forever young stuff...but think about it, your life is so boring! All you do is worship your own reflection. You feed off of other people's life force, which makes you monstrous. If it weren't for the people you feed off, then you wouldn't be pretty forever. You live in a half-life...a boring, broken, shadow. I reject your offer, and I reject you!"

She looks stunned and an icy look falls over her face, "An unexpected answer!"

The Wurdlacs are coming in closer waiting to see what happens next. Captain Vladislav inches closer and asks, "Should we...?"

She waves her hand at him, "Ugh, do I really need to say it?"

They start to move forward and all bare sharp, pointy, beautiful white teeth.

They crowd both sides of the long dining table. There seems to be no way to get past them to the door. Then I have an idea.

"Katya, what would little David do?" I quickly whisper urgently to her.

She catches on to what I'm saying and she grabs Elliot's hand and pulls him downward in his chair. There is a frantic commotion as Elliot, Katya and I dive under the dining table and quickly crawl down the length of the table to the door. The Wurdlacs are momentarily confused at this sudden turn. They have to scramble around the big table, knocking over chairs as they go. We crawl quickly to the end of the table, out the doors and bolt outwards. We are being chased by a mob of pretty people. We run as fast as we can down the confusing mirrored corridor. We see the Wurdlacs spill out of the dining room. Frighteningly, they seem to be gliding as if their feet are not touching the ground.

We run as fast as our feet can carry us. The Wurdlacs are hot on our tails. We burst out of the main dining hall doors to the outside. Our feet pound the ground kicking up dust clouds from the dry parched soil. I shoot a look over my shoulder and see the Wurdlacs are floating forward without kicking dust from the ground. Yacov is running ahead of us and looking over his shoulder barking loudly as if he is saying, run faster, run faster!

Above us I see the shimmering bubble blocking a heavy thunderstorm that is churning above. The black boiling cumulous clouds above make the streets dark. The reflecting buildings make it even more confusing. Out of the corner of my eye I see the aquamarine dome we had spotted before glowing softly like a beacon.

I yell to Katya and Elliot, "To the colored dome, maybe we can hide there!"

We sprint even faster until we are in front of the aquamarine colored dome. Elliot opens the door and we tumble inside, slide the door shut with a thud and lock it just in time. There is a thudding on the door as the fastest Wurdlacs bang on it and rattle the handle.

Inside to our surprise the dome is empty except a single orb floating in the middle of the air. The orb is perfectly spherical, and was about as big as our barn lantern. The inside is transparent with a blue haze sinking on the bottom. The top of the sphere looked as if it was raining inside and was rippling the haze. Katya shivers, "what is this weird place for?"

Elliot shrugs, "Art museum?"

She smirks and says, "Well, if this is the art museum then the curator must be extremely picky!"

I walk over to the edge of the aquamarine dome. These walls are not reflecting glass like the other Wurdlac buildings and are opaque. I touch the curved dome wall. The feeling is smooth and cold, like ice, but also stingy, like pins and needles. I walk away from the wall and walk towards the orb; it makes sort of a pinging noise as if it is working very hard.

Katya speaks, "Wow, this place looks important, there is only one thing in here."

The Wurdlacs pound on the door shouting, "do not touch the Sacred Orb!"

Hearing that, I smile, "Yes, it must be important."

I observe it more carefully and state, "It seems to have the same raindrop patterns as the strange shiny bubble above the village."

I hear Zmeya say, "If you lay one finger on the Sacred Weather Orb!"

That makes me wonder if I can touch the sphere.

As my finger nears the roiling colored sphere a bright blue spark leaps out to my finger from the sphere and stings me. I turn to my friends, "Anyone got any smarter ideas?"

Katya takes out her bow and puts an arrow in place; "I don't need to touch it in order to destroy it.

Elliot shouts out, "If you let us go, then we will leave your precious artwork alone."

Zmeya speaks angrily, "Idiot, it is not artwork! It is much more precious to us. Now I have a deal to make, come out and we kill you! And I promise your death will be quick and painless. Or, we can take all the time we need, and that will be a long, long time"

Elliot yells out again, "No deal, powder face!"

Zmeya speaks once more, "My last and final offer. I will turn you all into Wurdlacs, even the ugly ones."

Elliot snips, "Hey, don't call my friends ugly!"

I say, "No deal Zmeya! We all would rather die than be Wurdlacs."

Zmeya answers coldly, "That's okay, there never was a deal you idiot child. I was just stalling you so Captain Vladislav could fetch me the key to the dome. You children went from entrée, to amusement, to annoyance, and now to your end."

There is a loud click as the door slips open and Zmeya walks in looking enraged. An angry crowd of Wardlucs crowd outside the dome peering in to see what is happening.

She stops short when she sees Katya's bow aimed the glass ball.

Zmeya looks worried, "Put the bow down" she says in a stern voice. "You can't hurt me with a simple arrow".

I say sternly, "I know your weakness. My babushka told me stories about Vampire people that terrorized her. You came from Nikuda, you must have been the one that scared her so but was scared off by a simple bucket of water. Wurdlacs! A hard rains going to fall!!! Take the shot Katya!"

Katya aims with determination. Her fingers release on the

string as the arrow goes flying and the feathers brush her cheek. The arrow hits the orb in the dead center and it shatters to millions of glass shards and blue sparks. It makes the sound of one thousand clouds making thunder. The power is so great that it throws us to the ground. Then I hear a tremendous popping noise above. Suddenly the heaviest downpour I had ever seen falls from the sky. When the heavy raindrops hit the Wurdlacs they scream in agony. The skin on the Wurdlacs instantly start to boil and wrinkle. Then, their bodies collapse to the ground in piles of dust. As the dust dissolves in the water, a blue glow is released and forms into the shape of a body and then vanishes into nothingness. I feel these tortured souls are finally at peace. Still shaken and ears still ringing, I grab Katya and Elliot's arms and pull them outside in the pouring rain as Zmeya groggily stands up. She glares at us from inside the dome. I can see she wants to jump out of the dome and grab us, but the rain is falling down hard and she does not dare.

She gasps; as she looks upon the Wurdlac people she knew who were caught in the sudden downpour of rain and screams in fury. "I will get you for this!" she says cowering in the dome doorway. I look around and saw glowing diamond eyes of a few survivors in the doorways of the nearby mirror homes. They also don't dare come out of the building into the pouring rain. Elliot takes out his dagger, "Should we finish them off? There are still a few left, all we need to do is punch some holes into the roofs of the houses and let the rain do the rest."

I sigh, "Elliot, that would make us as horrible as the Wurdlacs."

He shrugs and puts the dagger back.

Katya shivers, "Let us please keep moving, I like the thought of being far away from here as possible. We don't

know how long the rain will last"
I nod, "On with our journey!" and away we go

18 THE WIZARD'S COTTAGE

We hike a day and a half, until the surrounding area is covered with trees. We see the start of a rough pebble stone pathway, about two oxcarts wide. It is made up of pressed down gray, black and white stones. The stones are rough edged and some had a burnt look like charcoal, as if they were from a fire pit. This road is not on the map Elliot had shown to me, making me think perhaps we were lost. We walk several miles down this stone path through the deep sun dappled forest.

 Elliot is blabbering about how close we must be, and keeps looking at the map he has. He shows me on the map the nearby mountain range, which we can see to the North, and points his finger at a picture of a huge stone tower on the map.

"Elliot, if were close, why don't we see this huge stone tower?" I ask suspiciously.

"Be patient" Elliot says.

"You're telling *me* to be patient?" I ask. "That's a new one".

Elliot gives me a withering look.

Katya offers up weakly, "Maybe it's invisible? Wizards probably don't like uninvited guests! Maybe we should head back home?"

I can tell Katya is still shaken up by Baba Yaga's house and the Wurdlacs.

Elliot looks annoyed at this suggestion. "If we look long enough, we can find it, even if it's invisible."

Katya mumbles, "Just because you want something badly enough, does not mean you will find it."

We keep walking for another few miles until mid-day. I am about to say something about being lost when Elliot speaks out, "THERE IT IS!"

Ahead we see an old cottage and next to it some stone ruins. He dashes ahead with determination but in his haste, he trips on a rock. I grab his arm in mid fall and heave him up. He blushes, brushes himself off, and keeps walking forward, but in a slower pace being careful of the many large scattered rocks around the cottage area.

I scan around to try to get familiar with my surroundings. The cottage is set in a clearing in the woods next to the foothills of the nearby mountains. The building is made of wood, except for the roof, which is made of straw. The lawn looks a bit rundown with weeds and long grass. Behind the cottage, looming over it is a large stone structure, which looks like a big base of a tower.

I nudge Katya, "What do you think that is?"

She looks at me and says, "I think its part of the tower from Elliot's map, or what used to be a tower at least."

I nod, that tower looked like it's seen better days, its large stones are weathered, burnt and cracked. The whole structure looks like it has been jaggedly shorn off, like a tree felled by an axe.

The tower is large, probably quadruple the width of the house, but the height was roughly cut off at about the two-story mark. Surrounding the base of the tower is a bit of rubble, but the rest is just missing.

We keep walking down the pebble stone path and reache the cottage. Elliot gets there before us and is reading something posted on the door. I walke to the door and see a stone tablet on the door, with a delicate cursive handwritten message, that reads, 'OUT TO LUNCH'. I groan. He was out to lunch? Is that even possible for a wizard to be out to lunch?

I was upset and so was Elliot. We didn't have time to wait while we had family members who were dying and the only one to cure the disease is out to lunch!

Yacov whimpers, and howls, "Awooooo!". Yacov seems to sense how upset I am. He looks very sad.

I pat Yacov on the back and try to comfort him. I knock loudly at the door for a while, to no avail, there is no answer.

I am getting angry, this was worse than getting my best dress dirty! I pound on the door again.

Katya offers, "maybe we should wait a little, I mean we don't want to get him angry"

I pat her on the back and say, "Katya you have a point, but we can't wait forever, I mean our family members are dying, and if we wait we might comeback and Svita and Alexey will be dead, you don't want that to happen do you?"

Elliot shrugs, "Fine let's wait for a few minutes for the wizard to finish his lunch".

We sit down on a rock nearby the cottage and wait.

"Why are we waiting, "Elliot says impatiently. "We should just walk in and get the potion."

"We agreed to wait", Katya mentions.

"The door looks locked," I say, "what do you want us to do, break the door down?"

"If that's one of our options, we should." Elliot says.

"That would make us rude like the Czar's Cossacks

97

breaking down our doors looking for taxes." I caution.

"The Czar's men are protectors and friends to our village." Elliot says proudly.

"Protectors? Feh!" I react. "The only thing they protect is our taxes!" I say angrily.

"You know, I won't even argue with you" Elliot says annoyed. He walks away, sits down, and starts stacking rocks and stones on top of each other.

"I think that was a little mean," Katya says softly

"I'm being mean? You like the Czar? You like them taking your taxes and pushing your family around!" I snap at her

"Natasha, watch your temper, we are all a team remember?" Katya mumbles

"Fine! Why don't you play with rock piles like your friend Elliot" I say in a pouty voice

"Actually maybe I will until you simmer down" She says and walks away from me sitting next to Elliot. She starts making the rock pile pyramids too.

I can hear them talking, probably about my temper, which I don't like. I sit on the ground and fume for some time. I feel bad I have lost my temper.

I keep walking around the cottage and bump into a large gray boulder. I look up and see it is part of the rubble made by the tower, from where I am standing it looks so tall it makes me feel tiny. It reminds me of being little and made me think about clutching mother's hand and when I would hide under her apron while she cooked. Suddenly, I miss Mother and hope they are not all worrying too much at home. If I close my eyes, I can imagine the smells of the kitchen at home and my Mother's cooking.

I walk into the big arch and just stand underneath, looking at how tall it is. It is probably as tall as two or three of me. I step inside the door and look up in awe at how big the tower must have once been, like what the map had shown.

There is a grey marble floor and many more arches; there are stairs that spiral up until the area where the tower was destroyed. I am amazed, who could have built it? Then I remember, oh yeah, it is probably the annoying wizard.

I walk back to the front part of the cottage; Elliot and Katya are still sitting silently playing with the stones.

"I'm sorry, I shouldn't have blown my top, that was very rude."

Elliot looks up and says, "apology accepted" and looks back down.

I sit down next to Katya in silence, watching what they are doing; stacking loose rocks into little piles balanced one flat rock on top of another. I start to make a pile with the rubble stones and soon find I am making pile after pile. It is fun and passes the time as we all work wordlessly piling stones about. I feel like I have made enough when I am surrounded with small rock piles. I am about to speak out when Elliot takes the words out of my mouth, "I think we all have waited long enough -don't you think so people?"

I nod; this wizard sure takes time eating.

We try the main cottage door, but it is still locked. The door looks pretty solid. I lead them to the little area behind the cottage that I found and they gasp at the remains of the tower and the staircase winding upwards to what is left of it. The stones making up the tower were the same color as the road pathway stones and look far older than the cottage.

19 MEETING THE GOLEM

We climb into the tower and over a big boulder. I vaguely hear mumbling echoing around the tower base. It is a deep voice that sounds like the very lowest note on a piano. The mumbling oddly is about math.

" Is QR to the fifth power, wait, I think, no! It's to the third, I should have known!"

We keep walking forward up the old grey crumbling tower steps, curious about the voice. We creep to the large wooden door at the top of the steps. The door seems to sag on its hinges, with great age. We hear pounding on a wooden table and the voice reciting math equations.

"He sounds upset" Katya mumbles. "We should leave, it must be a bad day for a visit." She shivers.

Ignoring her, I walk up to the door and knock. There is no answer. The door opens a crack and I step in. I look before me and see a massive hulk of a man sitting at a wooden stool before a large desk filled with papers. He seems to be made entirely of clay. He is at least eight feet tall and powerfully built. The clay man is wearing a large leather jacket and brownish pants. His clothing is old and patched at a number of places. The bottoms of his pant legs are frayed.

He stares at the many piles of papers on the desk with hazelnut colored large eyes. Something about the eyes is disturbing, he doesn't blink like you would expect. Something seems off. The papers have reams of numbers and equations on them.

He is bald and the top of his head is shiny clay. He has large ears, like they are shaped by hand out of clay, with not much skill in sculpting. His nose is large and almost beak shaped. His skin is reddish brown terra cotta colored clay. At first I thought he is a statue, but then he moves with a fluid manner.

I tremble; if this is the wizard, then I am very afraid. Elliot struts up to him, seeming to not notice his odd features, and shouts "Sir, I don't mean to disturb you but…"

The giant man booms back in his deep voice, "HA! Disturb me? Yes you disturbed me! I am in the middle of solving Euclid's parallel postulate, but you had to walk in and disturb me!"

He realizes then that we have inched backwards from him, afraid of what he might do.

"Oh, I'm sorry if I frightened you. I'm not used to having visitors in the tower. It is really nice to have someone to talk to. Can I get you some green tea and cookies?"

I ask timidly, "Are you Isaac Volshebnik? The scientist they call 'The Wizard'?"

The large clay man laughs a booming laugh, like the beat of a base drum. "No! I am not the wizard! I am a servant of the wizard. I am a Golem, actually I am THE Golem, but he has plans to make more. Many more of me."

"A golem?" I blurt out. "My Babushka told me legends of a golem, a mystical man shaped animated clay figure that saved a village in the story from bad people."

"Your Babushka is right on the money with a lot of these 'stories'" Katya whispers to me.

"What do you mean by many? Like five? Ten?" Elliot inquires.

"More like five hundred or thousands" The Golem replies proudly.

"Thousands?" I say. "Why would anyone need thousands of clay servants?"

"My Master has a vision that some day soon he will have an army of golems to replace all the boring labor that people do all day. He thinks that this will give people more time to think more."

Elliot nods in approval, "Well, my father would most likely approve of the idea of tireless, hard working servants."

Katya shakes her head, "One golem is ok, but imagine thousands of powerful golems doing all of our work for us? Where will that lead to?"

He looks at Katya in confusion, "But my master means well!"

She puts her fists on her waist and continues angrily, "Think of the few that can buy a golem at their fingertips, and the many others left in the cold, staring through the windows to peer at a golem serving a rich fat lazy person in a comfy warm room."

She turns to me and says, "Think! Your family's farm would be over because your farm would be taken over by a bunch of clay people working endlessly!"

I shiver to the thought of that. But she goes on, "And what if the Cossacks get a hold of these giants and use them as soldiers. Imagine, giant clay soldiers that can't get hurt! They could destroy a village in a few seconds!" This time Elliot shivers.

Golem nods fearfully, "And I would be the backbone of

the whole plan. I would be part of that army most likely! Not doing my beautiful math!"

Elliot speaks wistfully, "But the labor they could do! They would be such good maids or servants!"

Katya grimaces, "I don't suppose your dad would still pay human workers?"

"No, they would be comparably useless afterwards", Elliot agrees hesitantly.

"See! Look at this, and we are just beginning with the horrid possibilities!" Katya shouts.

I try to end this conversation by asking Golem a different question.

"What math are you trying to solve?"

He smiles suddenly, "only one of the most difficult problems of history! See, I am trying to solve this problem before some other mathematician does!"

I nod patiently, "Right. I still don't know what it is though"

He frowns, "Well, Euclid's parallel postulate states that if you have two lines whose sum is less than 180 degrees, they will meet in a certain area.

I nod, "ok, and?"

"Well, if the two angles both equal 180 degrees then they will never meet and they will always be parallel."

I nod in understanding; "So 180 in an angle to both makes it parallel?"

"Um, yes and no, see, if it was on a ball," he says, his large hands miming holding a sphere.

I cut him off, "It would meet on the other side, I see, well that is easy"

He nods his head, happy that I understand, "but can you put that into an equation?"

I shrug, "not really, maybe Elliot could since he's gone to school so many years."

Elliot looks at me funny, "I actually never really learned this, it seems a bit confusing."

Katya giggles, "Natasha, you learned more things than birdbrain does in school, your missing nothing!"

Yacov yips in agreement.

I nod, "that is true, I understood this before Elliot did!"

He blushes, "hey, I still know many things".

I laugh and tease him further, "like what? How to pick out a fancy cloak!"

Katya laughs, piling on, "or how to tie your shoes without a servant!"

Elliot starts to tear up, "you are both so mean, how can you live with yourself?"

I stop laughing, feeling bad I hurt Elliot's feelings.

Golem bends over and says to me, "does he do this face water thing every time you pick on him?"

I say, "No, he only does it when he feels like it."

He shudders, "he's seems very easily irritated"

I nod. Yacov looks up at the golem and starts to bark. The golem looks down at him and studies the dog.

"I envy you," Golem says out loud,

I smile, thinking he is referring to me, "Oh, you really don't have to admire me!"

He cuts me short, "no, I envy your dog."

I blush at the misunderstanding, "Oh, right, of course you would, not me."

He points at Yacov, "what's the dogs name?"

"Yacov"

Yacov yips to hear his name.

"The dog always has time to play." He says pleased.

I chuckle, "you would be surprised at what a hard working dog he is."

He smiles, then seems to remember we are there, "now, you came here because?"

I cough, "Right! You see, we came to this place to ask Isaac Volshebnik to give us a healing serum. The wizard seems to not be here, so perhaps you can help us"

He shakes his head, "I'm sorry but I'm not allowed in the cottage. I'm supposed to sit in the tower and plan an army of golems. I sadly have not made much progress because I have been distracted by wonderful math problems for a long time."

Katya smiles, "just tell us where it is and we can find it ourselves."

He sighs, "all the potions are held inside the magic cabinet."

"Uhm, magic cabinet?" I repeat skeptically.

He continues, "Yes, it may look ordinary next to the other cabinets, so find the one with dark red engraving on the side of the chest in Slavic. All the others are carved with Latin on the sides. Also, don't touch ANYTHING. My master has a bad temper. Here is a key to the cottage."

I look at Elliot with a stone face, "Hear that Elliot, DON'T TOUCH ANYTHING."

I take the key from the golem. The key is made of polished brass with strange markings on it. We make our way carefully back down the broken tower's stone staircase and back to the cottage door. I insert the key into the lock and it turns with a rusty squeak. I slowly push open the large wooden door and we all peer inside the cottage.

Inside I could hear a pin drop it is so quiet. The main room is pretty ordinary, chairs, a fireplace, candleholders, a small kitchen. The front room has a piano with sheet music piled on top. The curtains are drawn shut making the place dark inside. It is fairly tidy inside.

Behind a curtain is the room of chests that the golem mentioned. I walk carefully into the room and start looking for the one with the red engraving. Elliot calls out from the end of the row, saying, "I think I found it!"

I run down the isle with Katya by my side, her long hair flowing like water. We run to Elliot and I say, a little short of breath, "You said you found it, show us."

He points at a cabinet that has red engravings on the side. I nod, "Yup, this must be the one"

Katya looks at the cabinet from all different angles, "It doesn't look so special." She declares.

I walk around it and start to open a drawer. However, Katya slaps my hand away and hisses, "don't touch anything! Remember what the golem said?"

Then, unexpectedly, I hear a metallic slurred voice coming from the drawers. "Hey, I don't know ya, where are youse from?" the voice says with a peculiar accent.

I step back and whisper to Elliot, "Did the cabinet just talk?"

He nods slowly, "I think so" and steps back in shock.

Katya jumps a bit and says, "Let's get out of here! I don't like when *things* start to think!"

I hold her shoulder; "Look, a talking cabinet is the least freaky thing we have seen in the last week, so chill out."

The cabinet shakes a little and says, "Yeah, I can tawk, what's it to you?"

I speak as clearly as I can, "I don't usually hear talking cabinets"

It coughs, "Oh yeah? Well I don't usually see youts here! Now, I ask ya, where youse from and why are youse hear?"

I nudge Elliot to speak; he steps forward and says quietly, "Well, we came here because we need healing potions."

The cabinet answers reluctantly, "I only have one vial left, and the potions take a long time to make. I'm not going to give it away lightly. But, maybe youse could pay for it."

Elliot takes five gold coins from his pocket; each has a imprint of the Czar on it. The cabinet shrugs, "what will I do with money? I can't go anywhere."

Elliot looks sad; "money sure comes in handy when you need to buy stuff"

It speaks again, "Good point kid! Let me check my drawers and see what I need. Maybe I need something that you have."

The cabinet drawers open and close one by one, as the voice said, "let me see, I have lizard tails, toe fungi, dead leeches, live leeches, powcupine quails, Slavic dragon scales, parchment paper, five locks of black hair, four locks of blond hair, three locks of brown hair, two locks of white hair, one lock of grey hair, and, oh, would you look at that, no locks of red hair."

Katya looks up startled, "Wait, did you say red hair?"

The Cabinet answers, "Why yes I did, do you happen to have some red hair?"

Katya reluctantly says, "I have red hair"

Elliot pipes up, "and I have a dagger with me!" he says brandishing his blade from its scabbard.

Katya stands back as he comes closer, "Don't cut all my hair off!"

He rolls his eyes, "only a lock or two"

She grabs the dagger from him, "You know what, let me do it"

With that she slowly cuts off two locks of hair and places it in the open drawer. The drawer with the hair snaps shut. Then, another drawer slowly opens, with a single glowing flask in the drawer.

"Well, here is the potion, I advise you that the whole bottle is given to one person, and that they drink it all at once. Oh, and don't swim or ride a horse for at least 30 minutes."

Elliot looks at me with an odd expression on his face. I know that he really wants to have the potion, but later we can sort these things out.

The Cabinet sighs, "Well, I hope you will stop by again, I usually am not needed so this was fun! Goodbye!"

Katya waves and says, "Thanks cabinet!" as we head out the door.

I shiver; I didn't like seeing inanimate objects being alive, it makes me feel strange. I cradle the glowing flask and see a blue fluid inside. I wrap it in a bit of cloth padding and slip it into my jacket pocket.

Once outside, we see the golem sitting on a large rock waiting for us.

Elliot shakes the golem's finger and says, "Good luck on the golem army thing, I hope you can rebel against the man."

"Thank you! Your such a kind giant golem!" I say to the golem and proceed back down the crushed stone path away from the cottage and tower.

"Wait!" he yells after us, "Please, let me come with you!"

We turn around and Katya says, "What? Seriously?"

"I want to come with you! I thought for a while about what you all said to me. I don't want to stay here and help the wizard make an army of golems! He won't be able to easily make all these multiple golems without me. "

Elliot shrugs, "Maybe the big guy could be protection? Who knows what other stuff we might run into?"

I can see Golem really wants to come with us. "Okay, come on then!" Golem lumbers over and we start to walk home.

20 CAMPING IN THE WINTER WASTELAND

We head back home, but venture further North on the way back, to avoid going near the Wurdlac village again. We are not that far north, but the trees are covered in frost and the ground has fresh snowfall around. That is Russia for you, the weather changes often and mostly for the colder.

Elliot complains about the cold. Katya is humming and happy that we are heading for home finally. We hike for the entire day. The golem keeps talking about math problems. To my surprise, I actually enjoy the whole math discussion. There is something so pure and clean about math compared to the messiness of the world. The golem seems very pleased to be teaching math concepts.

We find a clearing nearby a large lake that is mainly clear of snow and decide to camp here for the night. Elliot gets out his map and studies it.

"The bad news is we maybe went too far north" He says concerned. "It looks like we already passed north of the village of Sakher and Sven's inn. The good news is we also skirted past most of the dark forest and this must be Long Lake. It's a fishing lake, but it looks mostly frozen over now. Were getting close to home actually." He says with a smile.

"Elliot, Natasha, thank you, again for helping me." Katya says, feeling happy.

I walk over to her, "Well, at least we are all still alive" and sit down next to her.

"Can we walk across the frozen lake?" Katya asks.

"No, that does not sound safe, even if it would be faster." I caution.

Elliot agrees, "Yes, I remember my father mentioned that drunk old Fyodor Karamazov walked out on the frozen lake one night and fell through the ice. That idiot's sons had to go and rescue him. The whole bunch of them almost drowned. We will have to take the long way around rather than risk the ice thickness."

Elliot whines, "Natasha, can you start up a fire? I'm freezing to death here."

I groan, "Do I always have to?"

He nods, "Yes, I don't know how!" and spoke again, "I already give food to you guys, you should be happy with your job"

I snarl and walk into the forest. As I was there I grab all the wood I can carry and run back, I didn't like taking any more chances. I quickly walk back to the camp and Elliot is making us all yummy food.

I laugh, "We aren't at a restaurant you know" and start to chow down the food.

Katya says, "shouldn't we make the fire a little smaller, it could attract animals." Elliot pipes up, "No I think we should make it larger so that we have more light to see and we could be warmer!"

"Smaller." Katya hisses.

"Larger" Elliot repeats.

"Smaller."

"Larger!"

"Smaller!"

I speak up, "neither, its good how it is." They shrugged, "but it's so cold!" Elliot whines.

"You're such a wimp."

Katya laughs.

"Hey! That's not true!" Elliot says making a pouty face.

I laugh, "In your dreams."

Katya jerks her head up, "look!"

I shoot my head up to where she is pointing, "What? More danger?" Maybe the fire is too big?

She giggles, "No, it's just a shooting star." She closes her eyes and whispers something.

Elliot smirks, "that's so illogical, you can't wish upon a star that falls. It is like wishing on a fish that went into the air and is diving back in."

She grunts, "Some people Elliot, can believe what they want"

"Whatever, it's illogical anyway you put it"

I laugh, but then lie down and look up at the black sky, with stars gleaming like candles far away. I wonder if there were other people doing Sabbath far away. I nudge Elliot, "hey, do you think that there are people in the sky lighting Sabbath candles?"

Elliot scoffs, "these questions you ask are the reasons that you can't go to school."

Golem speaks up after hearing our conversation, "actually Elliot, I think her questions are deep and reasonable, and these are the signs of a true scholar."

I smile hearing this. Could I really become some kind of scholar?

Golem sighs, "I wish I could teach, there is no greater blessing than to teach young minds."

Elliot rolls his eyes, "A golem as a teacher? That's ridiculous!"

I nod, remembering what my father had said about woman rabbis, "almost as ridiculous as an orange on a Seder plate." Elliot groans, "This is the most boring topic I have ever heard of. I am going to sleep, don't wake me up for any reason." And with that he went to his blanket and snores heavily.

Katya smiles, "I guess he is not first on watch duty!"

I tell Katya to get some rest. I sit up listening to the others sleeping and poke at the fire. I watch the stars turning in the sky above the tree line. After several hours I know its Katya's turn to watch out, but I let here sleep more. She looks so peaceful curled up in her blanket, her red hair framing her face. The stars begin to dim after a few hours and the sky reddens on the eastern horizon. I'm used to seeing this sunrise sky when I get up before dawn to do my chores back in Nikuda. It makes me actually miss waking up at home. On the other hand I feel very changed by this adventure and wonder if I can get back into the slow routine of my old life.

Katya is stirring from her resting place and sits sleepily next to me.

"Natasha, you should have woken me up for watch! Have you slept even a little?" She says concerned.

"I'm fine, really." I calm her.

Out of the corner of my eye I think I see something move in the deeper forest just beyond the light of the campfire.

Katya touches my shoulder, "What is it?"

"Nothing, I think it was just my imagination"

"Really, whenever we think that- something evil with bad teeth pops up."

"I guess you are right, maybe we should prepare for the worst"

"This is true, as my momma once said, when a bear is looking for honey, it runs when it hears the buzz, not when it feels the sting."

"You better get your bow"

"Are you kidding, it hasn't been farther than arm's reach ever since Baba Yaga's hut"

"Okay, wake up Elliot and the golem and keep alert!"

21 THE WINTER WOLVES

"Did you hear that?" I ask Katya; she quickly turns around and sees two yellow gleaming eyes staring from the edge of the woods. I quickly turn around and I see more sets of eyes around us. It was some kind of a wolf. First two appear, then ten! There is swirling snow and it is hard to see where the snow ends and where they begin.

It is a frightening sight to see in the flickering firelight. They all seem to take shape emerging out of the dark forest. The wolves come closer, howling a low sound that you almost feel more than heard. It is a low moan of sorrow and coldness. It is scarier than anything so far!

I want to run away, but I don't think we can outrun or outfight these winter wolves.

The golem hears the low moan and nods his head, "Ah! I recognize that sound, I'm pretty sure the master made creatures like that in his laboratory. They were results of a failed experiment that got loose a while ago. They must have tracked us from the tower area."

"What are they?" I ask hurriedly.

"I really don't know, " the golem admits. "I really focused on my math and kind of ignored the master's other experiments".

Katya squeals, "He had other experiments besides you?"

Elliot yells over the howling wind, "can we focus on the task at hand?"

I nod in agreement and say, "Elliot, I need you to take left wing on my side, no buts!"

I run to the golem, he seems disconcerted.

"I don't like all this fighting, maybe we can give them a peace treaty?"

"NO! That is not happening! They seem to be creatures of the ice; can they even talk?"

The golem shakes his head, "I think just growl and kill, so yeah, not as friendly as Yacov."

I immediately respond, "That is totally the understatement of the year."

The wolves come closer, every step sounds like a plate smashing to the ground. Katya cowers behind me, clutching her bow.

As I look around I see that these wolves are transparent! You can see their hearts pumping, there brains thumping, and most disgusting, the arteries were turning blue and red, blue, red, blue, red and on and on. It is quite revolting. They even have shiny icicle teeth.

These horrible ice beasts are not our only problems. As we back away from the wolves closing in on us, I realize we are near the edge of the frozen lake. I have sort of picked this place to camp because the frozen lake was pretty. Now I regret it. We walk back slowly, making sure that we do not step onto the frozen lake surface. They are closing in.

"I'll save you Natasha!" I hear the golem yell. All the wolves turn to his direction; he looks very frightened, but starts to fight them off. He takes one by the leg and gives it a good swing. He definitely is as strong as he looks. The wolf launches towards another and they collide. However, the two merge together suddenly into an even bigger ice wolf. That didn't help.

The golem looks in shock; his unblinking eyes are glazed with fear. The wolves circle around him, and breathe out blasts of ice breath. At first only the bottoms of his feet are solid ice, but then the ice crawls over him, turning him into an ice statue. We all look in shock, the wolves look like they are not done yet, and they start to look my way. The wolves inch closer and closer and I start moving more and more back. We have no choice but to back out onto the frozen lake, although we don't really know how solid it is.

"You guys cross the frozen lake, I will stay here on this side and distract the wolves!" I shout.

I really should have moved to the side. I thought that I should think about other things about life, like my poor, sweet brother all alone and sick. Wait! I should give the potion to Elliot!

"Hey Elliot! Catch this and run while I distract the wolves" I throw the blue bottle to him, and pray he will catch it. He catches it and slips it into his cloak.

"What should I do with this?"

"Run with it! The wolves are busy with Yacov and me!"

I can see the fear and horror in his eyes. The wolves are growling at me, and I can feel the cold radiate off of them.

The ice under Elliot and Katya's feet is crackling and brittle, but it holds. I can see the lake water sloshing under the ice. I hope it will hold until they pass over to the other side of the lakeshore.

I wave around a torch from the fire, which manages to hold the wolves back, giving my friends more time to get across.

Katya and Elliot have made it to the far shore of the frozen lake. Katya shoots a few arrows at the wolves, but they seem to deflect off their ice hides.

"Natasha! What about you? We cannot leave you!" Katya screams

"No, just leave! Run with Elliot! Don't look back my dear friend! Remember me!"

"Nooooo!" Katya screams again futilely firing a few more arrows, until Elliot grabs her around the waist and drags her away from the lakeside.

This was horrible, that I might be killed near a pond with monstrous ice wolves eating me, plus my brother dying so far from here.

"Arf! Arf!" I see Yacov jump into the way as the double sized wolf lunged at me. I am afraid they are going to eat him whole in one icy bite. He shoots around them like a furry meteor, and catches all their attention. Then like a bolt he tears across the frozen lake with the whole pack of wolves in hot pursuit. They seem to have forgotten me entirely.

"Do be careful Yacov!" I shout with horror on my face. My brave loyal dog has saved me.

He races across the ice, bouncing across the ice like a skipping stone. I hear heavy cracking noises as the huge weight of the wolves hits the frozen pond surface. Just as Yacov reaches the far shore, the lake surface buckles with a crash under the weight of the giant wolves and dumps them all into the deep cold black water. The wolves are so cold that it almost instantly freezes the lake over again, trapping them into a solid prison, frozen from surface to the bottom of the lake.

Yacov yips with joy. I am so happy my eyes well up with tears. Yacov bounds into my arms. I am so proud that my little pup saved me.

I run over to Golem encased in the ice block. Using the camp axe I free the bottom of the ice block from the ground and now I can easily slide the ice block like it was on wheels. I push the frozen Golem next to the campfire, where he starts to thaw. I wait until the ice melts away. I hope Golem is not dead, but he looks so motionless, like a big clay statue. Then suddenly his arm moves and he animates again. He looks a little chilly but seems to be recovering slightly.

I hear crunching in the snow and I whip around, the axe in my hand. More wolves? No, I'm delighted to see Elliot and Katya show up and run into my arms.

"Are you ok?" questions Katya; she gives me a tight squeeze around my waist.

 I hug her back, "yeah, I just got a couple of scratches."

Elliot mutters, "at least she didn't fall into the water, what a klutz."

"I'm sorry Natasha, we were heading towards Nikuda and I decided we could not leave you alone, so we headed back."

We hug again, both of us crying.

 Suddenly, Golem cracks out of the remaining ice and falls backwards with a groan.

"Golem, are you ok?"

"I'm fine. It was a nice nap in the ice block."

I tap him on the shoulder, "You, have a little ice in your ear"

He smiles, "that's ok, it will melt" and we proceed again towards home.

22 RETURN TO THE DEEP FOREST

We sit down cramming together at the fire. Katya is shaken with everything so I hold her and comfort her as best I can. Elliot is sitting alone.

"What's wrong Elliot, were almost home."

He sniffs, "I know."

I walk over to him and sit next to him as he broods over the fire.

"Hey, I know your sad, tell me why."

He sniffs again, "What if my mom already died? We have been gone for awhile."

I shudder at the thought of Alexey already dying. Why did Elliot always think of these things?

"I know how you feel be we can only take our chances." I comfort.

He grimaces,

"But I hate taking chances" and starts to sob on my shoulder.

I hug him back, "sometimes, I hate taking them too, but we have to go home, no matter if our family is dead or not."

He looks up at me,"I know you don't feel so bad right know but when you come home and your brother is dead, what will you do?" He looks at me.

Oy! I think about it, "I will have to live, love, and move on."

He shrugs, "that's what you say now, but wait till you come home."

I place my hands on my hips and say, "Hey, are you implying that my brothers already dead and I should just prepare now?"

He shakes his head, "no, I'm just saying" he stops, and walks away.

I walk over to Yacov and start to pet him. His silky hair is waving in the wind and his tongue is sticking out.

"Do you understand what I'm going through?" I tell Yacov. He looks up and whimpers,

"That's right Yacov, I am sad."

He places his paw on my hand and lies down beside me.

"Are you sad?" Golem says behind me. I nod.

"Why would you be sad, Natasha?"

I look up at his clay brown eyes, "Because for all I know my brother might be dead."

He tilts his head, "But do you really know that?"

I shake my head, "I guess not."

He bends over, "Sometimes, I like to think about happy things when I am sad, like complex math!"

He smiles, "You really can't tell the future if you haven't seen it yet"

I shrug, "I guess you're right none of us can predict the future."

He nods, "I tried to predict the future, the math is too difficult even for me!"

I walk away to Katya who is now poking on the fire with a stick and talking to herself.

I walk over to her once more and say "Hey Katya, how are you?"

She turns her head, "the same" and continues to poke the fire.

I take another stick and poke with her. "Are you still shaken up about the Wardlucs, Baba Yaga, or the ice wolves?"

She nods. "Pick one or any combination!"

"I don't remember you being so afraid of things!" I say

She looks at me and says, "Worst. Vacation. Ever." and gives a faint smile.

She continues, "at least chopping wood and peeling potatoes will seem like a paradise compared to what we went through."

I smile, "I can't say your wrong." And I lie down and stare at the beautiful lights in the sky.

23 ELLIOT LEAVES

Elliot could not sleep all night. He sat near the dying embers while Natasha and Katya sleep behind him. Golem was snoozing in the corner murmuring math, "Every simply connected…closed 3-manifold… is homeomorphic to the 3-sphere…its beautiful…"He mumbles in between snores.

Elliot waves his hand in front of Golem's face to check if he is awake. But he seems to be in a deep math slumber. Elliot snorts, *even the clay lump gets his rest while I ponder on what to do.*

The small blue glass flask shimmers under his cloak, warm against his chest. Natasha had thrown it to him when they were fighting against the winter wolves and forgot to take it back.

Or, is it because she trusts him?

The idea gnaws at him. His hair wisps in the wind, he can't believe he is still alive after all they went through. He thinks his parents will be proud. His parents? What do his parents think is happening now; they must be worrying about him, hoping he is still alive.

Suddenly the thought jolts his mind, is mother still alive? Was this trip all for nothing? How is Natasha so sure that a half dose will work? The cabinet did say that only a full dose will mend any illness. He sighed and looked at the bottle. *It's just so tiny,* he thought, *I've gone through all this…what if the half doses end up with both of them dead! That would be a sick joke. This is a dilemma that even king Solomon would have trouble figuring out. But, they are going to wake up soon.*

It is nearly dawn, and the group is still fast asleep. The stars above shiver and rotate during the night and Elliot knows he doesn't have much time to make a choice now. When they wake, there will be no choosing. A part of him wants to wake Natasha and talk about it, but he pushes that thought away. *Alexey's just a chimneysweeper, and my Mom is the heart of this whole community! She always gives clothes to the less fortunate. And she is so nice, like when I was busy studying she chopped wood for me. He pauses in horror, is that really how she got sick? Is this all my fault? I have to save her no matter what!*

Elliot slowly stands up. He stretches quietly and then quickly rolls his sleeping bag up and places it in his backpack. He silently gathers his belongings. Elliot places half his remaining food in a neat pile next to the fire. He places his pack on and creeps past the sleeping girls, being careful not to wake them up. The flask is hot against his chest. He looks back one more time at his sleeping friends and slips off into the night. He departs a few hours before Natasha wakes up.

24 SVITA'S FINAL LESSON

Elliot trudges through the night, his path lit by the starry sky above and the waxing moonlight. He tries to recognize some of the constellations above, but can't recall which one is which. Natasha probably would remember he thinks. She seems to have the same sharp memory as her brother Alexey had when they were classmates.

He starts to recognize the familiar farms and houses of his village as he walks through the night. Several times he thinks about turning around but he maintains his resolve. He arrives back in downtown Nikuda just before dawn. He walks past all the sleepy shops and unlit homes. Reaching his home, he can see the crack of sunrise split the darkness and just begin to illuminate the outline of his home and the big oak tree in the front yard. He stands on the front step and takes in a deep breathe. *This is it! The moment to find out if this was the right thing to do!* He opens the door quietly and steps inside. It feels so nice to be home again. He puts his back against the thick door and just listens to the sounds of the house, the tick tock of the big grandfather clock in the entry hallway, the crackle of the fireplace.

He realizes he has to be very quiet because his father is sleeping on the couch. It must be to avoid Svita's dragon cough. His father is snoring lightly and mumbling while he sleeps. He thinks about waking his father, but he is in a rush to see if his mother is still alive. He tiptoes upstairs and into his mother's bedroom.

He walks into the room slowly to avoid letting the door squeak. He sees a small table near the door has been setup and it is filled with various pharmacy items and doctor's implements. There are several charts tracking the progress of the Dragon Cough. Father has not spared any expense in her treatment.

"Mother?" Elliot calls out hesitantly.

A raspy voice answers, "Elliot?"

He ran to the voice and there is Svita, lying in bed. There are bouquets of flowers all around from people who wish her well. She has her knitting gear on a chair nearby. She is making a sweater that looked like it would fit him.

He holds her hand gently, "Not feeling well Mom?"

"That's a silly question. Am I? I read your note and we didn't hear from you, so I assumed you were gone, my darling boy."

"Your not dying Mom, not for long!"

"What do you mean?" She says surprised.

"Just like my note said, I left for a while and came back with a cure for you!"

"You did?" she asks amazed.

"Well, I went with Natasha and Katya, you know, the girls who play with Vera all the time. Anyway, we went to a scientist guy's house to retrieve a serum, went through a lot of adventures together, and now I have it to cure you." Elliot said proudly, holding up the softly glowing blue glass vial.

"That's so wonderful Elliot! So Natasha got a serum to

cure her poor sick brother Alexey also?" She asks, sitting up in the bed.

Elliot looks at his feet, "About that, you see, I sort of took the serum for you so you could have a full dose, because I was afraid half a dose wouldn't work. We only have enough dose for one person. "

Svita gasps and coughs, "Why? Why would you do that, now Natasha has no serum for her brother Alexey!"

"Mother, he's just a chimney sweeper!" Elliot says angrily

"But he is also a family member" Svita objects.

"Not my family member." Elliot protests.

"But imagine if Vera was sick and Natasha took the serum for herself to give to her mother, how would you feel then?"

"Yeah...pretty bad"

"So give him a half of the dose and come back to me," She says   firmly.

"No" Elliot said, folding his arms in front of him.

There is a silence and then Svita sighs, "my baby boy, the last lesson for you, from your Mommy. Do what is right always, so you might attain a heart of wisdom forever. "

And as she mouthed out the word forever, she pauses, closes her eyes and passes away.

Elliot holds her hand, and as it turns warm to cold, he starts to cry. As he cries he thinks of all the possibilities to be ashamed of, in the past and future. He wants to smash the blue bottle, but his body will not let him, all it will let him do is sob.

Releasing her hand at last, he flees from his Mother's room, rushes to his room and throws himself onto his childhood bed, crying into his soft pillow. He lies in his bed, and thinks to himself, *what a horrible world*. He starts to doze off. He has a horrible dream, dogs are chasing him, there are only two, and they have sorrow in their eyes. He is holding the glowing blue bottle. He runs towards a simple farmhouse. Inside is a blond haired boy coughing and wheezing. Suddenly everything is slow motion. Ahead, there are two paths, one is a blue door, and one is red.

He does not know what any of this means, so he grabs the red door. The dogs are gone but the room makes him feels sad. Inside it is grey and black and many things are floating around him- like his lost boots, and his dead dog Sali. He reaches out to pet Sali but she vanishes before his hand touches her.

He went over to reach more things that were floating all around like fish in an aquarium. He looks and sees a younger version of his mother, she is cooing over to him. He ran into her arms, but as he did she disintegrates to dust, leaving a little puddle of a blue liquid like in the bottle. He hesitates to touch this item but he did anyway.

The liquid shivers and started to float as he sat down and falls through one of his beloved beds. The liquid becomes a mirror, reflecting lights all around. He looked into the mirror but instead of his reflection, he sees an image of Alexey repeating over and over which then fades into utter blackness. Eliott wakes with a start and exclaims, "I have to save Alexey because it's the only right thing to do." He says firmly. He runs downstairs as quickly and quietly as possible. He fills his half full bag again with provisions from the pantry and grabs a spare water canteen. "I think this is enough." He states and creeps by his father who is still fast asleep. He steps outside into the rising sunlight.

25 THE RETURN TO NIKUDA

I wake up and rub the sleep from my eyes. I am so tired after the battle with the Winter Wolves. I stretch my arms and felt a wincing pain in my shoulder. The memories of fighting the winter wolves are coming back as I am waking up. It's hard to believe we survived all that. I blink a little and slowly stand up. Katya is sitting on a rock that overlooks some nearby river. I sit next to her while drinking some water. "Good morning" I chirp, but she looks back at me clearly not happy.

I nudge her smiling, "not awake yet?"

Katya shakes her head, "No, I am awake as any day; but I have something to tell you…something that will displease you."

"What?" I say flatly.

"Elliot…"

I sighed, now what? "Yes? What about him?"

"Elliot is… gone."

My eyes dart over to Elliot's resting area. It is then that I notice his knapsack and blankets are missing. There is a neat pile of food next to the fire area. I briskly stand up and walk over to his spot.

I nervously laugh, "What…no…he must have got up early

and…and filled his canteen with water…or maybe he went to get firewood, perhaps…" my voice trails off desperately searching for a reason for why he is missing.

Katya sternly looks at me and says, "I have been up for awhile, right after the first rays of sun hit our campsite, and he was not here even then. I thought that he was retrieving something, so I waited for him. I waited and waited…but he did not come. Natasha, face the facts, he ditched us."

"Why would he leave without us?"

"Natasha, he has the healing vial, remember?"

"No…" I gasped.

I sink onto my knees, my eyes glazed with tears. I look around desperately; feeling suddenly lost and sick.

"Elliot!" I cry out, "Elliot, how could you! I trusted you! That potion was my brother's only hope of survival! After all we have been through? How could you!!"

I am now sobbing and punching the ground. Katya slowly approaches me with tears in her eyes, and hugs me.

There is a long silence until Golem slowly says, " Well, I'm not good at this human emotion stuff, but are we still going to Nikuda, or are we heading somewhere else?"

I stand up, wiping the tears away.

"Yes golem, we are still going to Nikuda." I say coldly. " I have some unfinished business with someone there."

Golem looks confused but smiles, "okay then, lets go," he says.

We quickly pack up our bags and head towards Nikuda.

As we walk to the edge of Nikuda, I feel some relief when I notice a familiar face. I see farmer Jonah working on his potato field. Jonah looks up, his steel grey eyes widen with confusion. Then, he looks terrified.

"Natasha! Behind you, a monster!" he calls and runs as quickly as he can into the fields.

Golem looks down at Yacov. Confused he says, "People

just don't understand dogs, do they?" and proceeds to lumber down the road.

I'm going to have to think of some way to cover Golem up more.

We reach the downtown of the village as the morning activity is just starting up. There are men delivering papers and milk to houses, and people opening doors to shops, the workers yawning at the welcoming sky. Children are heading out to their morning chores. The people seem to act normal, as if a wheel has still been turning, even without us. Although, you can never hide from the fact that every person we walk by stares at Golem, and clearly is in shock. After so many glances, I consider hiding Golem under a cloth, but then remember that Golem is eight feet tall and as wide as a bull.

Katya taps my shoulder, "Golem is getting a lot of stares. Maybe we can dress him up as something friendly, like a clown perhaps!"

I shudder, "An eight foot tall, five hundred pound clown? I would pee my pants even if I just glanced at that!"

Katya giggles.

I look over at a pile of wood and pick up a flat piece, some string and a chunk of coal and write in block letters on the board, "I AM NOT A MONSTER, I AM AN AMERICAN."

Katya looks at my sign and says, "ah, genius, but what if they know that Golem is not an American?"

"Do you know what an American looks like?"

"Ah, no."

"Then neither will these people! Okay Golem, come here"

Golem walks over to me and kneels down so I can put the sign around his neck.

I pat his shoulder, "try to act as American as you can"

Golem thinks about that and asks, "Do you think I should

strap on some guns and yell a lot?"

Katya shakes her head, "Please golem, we are trying to calm people, not scare them away!"

Golem hollers, "Ah reckon so!"

I roll my eyes, "Stop it"

He smiles, "You betcha!" and gives me two thumbs up.

As we proceed to walk people seem to jump in shock but calm down after reading the sign. Some people even say 'howdy' to him. Its working.

We reach my farmhouse, and we stamp the snow off our shoes as we slowly head inside my house. I can hardly speak as I see my parents jump up and run over to me.

"Natasha! Baby, my child, we thought you were dead!"

I break out in tears as we all hug, "Where, where is Alexey?"

They strain to talk, "He's in his room." My mother announces, looking very concerned.

Without waiting a second, I dash up the stairs. I can feel a sudden rush of fear as I enter to the sound of murmuring.

"Natasha?" He says weakly.

I jump to the side of his bed, and grab his hand. I am so glad it feels so warm. I cry as I speak, "your alive, how?"

He smiles, "a sad faced boy in a dark cloak was suddenly standing above my bed. I was feverish, so I could not even focus on the face. Honestly, I thought this must be the death angel come for me. He gave me a tiny glass bottle that was holding blue glowing liquid. He gave it to me without a word spoken."

I gasp, "It must have been Elliot!"

He sigh, "that's impossible, that snobby boy I knew from school, would never do something so generous to someone apart from his family."

I laugh with content, "he's changed since the last time you saw him."

"I better go back down to talk to Mom and Dad. I'm so glad you're healed. It's a miracle."

He stares at me, "do you like him?"

"Like who?"

"Elliot"

"No, that's crazy!"

Alexey pulls himself out of bed, "Its ok, I can walk again! I really feel amazing."

We both go downstairs. Mother and Father are both staring in shock at Katya and Golem.

"I don't know which part to be more shocked at, Katya alive again or this…thing" Father says wide-eyed.

"Yeah, I saved Katya in the Deep forest. It's a long story Papa! Oh and this is our new friend, he is a Golem."

"I know what a Golem is, I am a Rabbi you know!" Father says shortly. "Who is his master? A bad master makes a scary Golem" Father warns.

"I believe I have no master." Golem exclaims

"I'm not sure if that is more scary". Father says with worry.

"Father, he's very gentle and loves to do math and science." I object.

"Actually my dream is to be a teacher." Golem confesses.

Father smiles, "We actually are looking for a good teacher at the school, since Akiva Eiger is retiring."

Golem claps his large hands together happily.

I hug Katya, feeling happy. "Katya" I whispered.

"Yes?"

"I know what Elliot did."

"Yes?"

"He gave the serum to my brother."

"Really?"

"I know, I am surprised too, but that is what he chose!"

"So where is Elliot?"

We race over to Elliot's home. Victor opens the door and

tells us about Svita. Victor says that Elliot must have stopped there and that he had dropped a map accidently when he left. He shows it to us. On it is circled a lower left part of the map, a small island. I see in the corner a picture that seems fairly small and it says, 'BUYAN ISLAND'

Katya looks at me with awe, "do you think that is where he is going?"

I nod, "its worth a shot, anything, as you may know now, is possible. Also, he did save my brother from dying, sacrificing his mom instead. I think I owe him one."

"Do you want me to come with you?" Katya asks.

"Oh Katya, you need to go home!"

"No, we go together" Katya insists.

"Wait, just like that?" I say, surprised.

"Yes, I don't seem to have much to do now, so why not? I have a bow, food, and an amazing friend."

I smile, "well, lets pack our bags once more, no rest for the weary, as my father would say."

Katya looks out the window and sees golem talking and laughing with my father, "Should we bring golem with us?"

I nod, "Lets ask him. If he is his own master, he should choose not be ordered around."

Katya and I run over to talk to Golem.

"Well big guy, are you ready for more adventure?" I ask.

"Natasha, if it is okay with you, I want to stay in Nikuda and become a teacher. It has been my dream to teach students things like mathematics. When you return I hope I can teach you also, because I know you will be a great student."

I nod and shake his hand. My dream of becoming a student seems like it will come true.

"That sounds great! As soon as we go and retrieve Elliot, I will come right back to start lessons! I don't think I will be gone very long. With the amount of rest breaks Elliot normally takes when he travels, we should catch up to him in a few days time."

I take a moment to think back on my journey. I can't believe we survived all those dangers. I think about how I have changed over the course of this exciting adventure. I learned a lot about the importance of controlling my temper and thinking before acting. I think about Elliot and how my sense of him changed from a poor first impression to respect. I made new friends along the way that I never would have expected to call my companions. I also think Katya and Elliot have learned many things over the journey. Katya has grown more fearful during this trip, understandably given the things she has experienced. I do hope she can find her courage again. My mind then travels to the changes that will happen in the future. Mainly, that I will be a student in the Shtetl's Yeshiva. Not only this, but Golem will be a teacher there. The Talmud writes that one should "Find thyself a teacher". I seem to have done that.

I rejoin Katya and she states that she will go with me to find Elliot.

My mother and father start to protest about the danger of us traveling the open road when Alexey interrupts.

"Don't worry Papa! I will go with them and make sure they are safe!" Alexey promises. "I owe it to Elliot to find him and return him home. The guy did save my life."

I smile, very happy that my brother Alexey will be joining us for the journey to retrieve Elliot, "well then, destination Buyan Island!"

TO BE CONTINUED in Book 2: *HEART OF COURAGE...*

ABOUT THE AUTHOR

G.W. Roberts is a young author living in Massachusetts. In addition to writing G.W. loves fencing, reading, bicycling and board games.